Where was Daniel?

Mary Anna's blue eyes had been haunted with concern for three days, ever since she and Daniel had lost everything they owned to a renegade Indian's torch. It was a mercy Frances Gerald had taken them in. And Mary Anna was worried, too, about Daniel and her father. There was rumor about town that some of the men had banded together to raid the reservation in retaliation for all the attacks the Comanches had made on the white settlers.

Had Daniel and her father joined up with these raiders? Surely not. Daniel was an honorable man. Her father, too. No, she was sure they were just out hunting.

She put on a bright smile as she heard the hoofbeats of an approaching horse. "Boys, I think your father is coming in. Tump, help T.P. get washed up for supper." She wiped her hands on her apron and smoothed her hair as she opened the door. Her smile froze on her face. The incoming rider was slumped over his horse.

LINDA HERRING is the mother of four grown children and the wife of a minister. Her writing is an avenue of ministry whereby she both entertains and uplifts with her down-to-earth view of Christianity. In this latest addition to **Heartsong Presents**, Herring has used her family's history in Erath County, Texas, to create a powerful look into pioneer life on the western frontier.

Books by Linda Herring

HEARTSONG PRESENTS
HP49—Yesterday's Tomorrows
HP72—Song of Captivity

Dreams
of the Pioneers

Linda Herring

The Thornton Saga

Heartsong Presents

For Mary Anna Thornton Smith
who started the wheels turning

A note from the Author:
I love to hear from my readers! You may write to me at
the following address: **Linda Herring**
                              Author Relations
                              P.O. Box 719
                              Uhrichsville, OH 44683

ISBN 1-55748-773-1

DREAMS OF THE PIONEERS

Cover illustration by Kathy Arbuckle.

PRINTED IN THE U.S.A.

one

The Texas air blew cool, but Daniel Thornton's shirt was soaked with sweat born of fear as he hunkered down in the dense plum thicket. *Where are they?* he worried. He strained his ears for the slightest sounds that might give them away.

With a venomous whistle, an arrow sliced through the branches, just missing Daniel. *Over there.* He squinted, trying to pierce the thicket with his gaze.

"Hey! Come out, John. Come out. We won't hurt you," an Indian called, using the name they gave all white men.

Daniel knew that was a lie. Especially now. Now that he had done such a horrible thing to gain revenge from the Indians. The taste of bile rose in his throat at the thought of the atrocities committed by the Indians against white people.

He turned toward the voice and took careful aim with his Sharp's rifle. The gurgling scream that followed his shot told Daniel he had hit his target. *One down,* he thought. *But where are the other two?*

With the same deadly whistle, a second arrow flew from the opposite side, thudding into Daniel's elbow and laying the flesh open to his wrist. He ground his teeth to keep from screaming. He dared not move an eyelash. Two more exploratory arrows skimmed through the bushes at different angles, and then Daniel heard the welcome sound of unshod ponies riding off in the early twilight.

Daniel took off his bandanna and wrapped it tightly around his forearm, just above the entry wound. Then he waited to be sure the horses had ridden away. One thought kept him from passing out with pain and loss of blood: he must get back to

Mary Anna.

When he was sure he was alone, Daniel crawled out of the thicket and signaled to his horse. "Take me to town, boy. Home to Mary Anna." He slumped over in the saddle, holding on to the horse's mane. "Mary Anna, Mary Anna," he whispered. "Forgive me, Mary Anna."

ða

In the town of Stephenville, Mary Anna stirred a large kettle of stew over the hot coals of the fireplace. It was a worry to be cooking in someone else's kitchen, taking advantage of Frances Gerald's hospitality this way.

Mary Anna's blue eyes had been haunted with concern for three days now, ever since she and Daniel had lost everything they'd owned to a renegade Indian's torch. It was a mercy this good soul had taken them in. And she was worried, too, about Daniel and her father. There was a rumor about town that some of the men had banded together to raid the reservation in retaliation for all the attacks the Comanches had made on the white settlers.

Had Daniel and her father joined up with these raiders? Surely not. Daniel was an honorable man. Her father, too. No, she was sure they were just out hunting.

She put on a bright smile as she heard the hoofbeats of an approaching horse. "Boys, I think your father is coming in. Tump, help T.P. get washed up for supper." She wiped her hands on her apron and smoothed her hair as she opened the door. Her smile froze on her face. The incoming rider was slumped over his horse.

At twenty-two, Mary Anna had lived on the Brazos River frontier for two years, long enough to learn that she'd best be prepared for anything. Now she straightened to her full five feet two inches and did what had to be done. She ran out and grabbed the reins of her husband's horse, bringing horse and rider to a stop in front of the door.

Daniel's face was gray; he was unconscious. An arrow stuck out of his arm, and a blood-stained bandanna was wrapped tightly around his forearm.

"Whoa, boy. Daniel! Can you hear me?" Frantically she looked for signs of life. Daniel's eyelids flickered, raising Mary Anna's hopes. "Hold on to me. I'll help you into the house." *Thank You, Lord, for bringing him back to me.* Then she turned toward the house and shouted, "Frances, help me!"

A handsome, grandmotherly woman came hurrying out, a frown of concern on her face. "Is he alive?"

"Barely."

Between them they dragged, supported, and carried Daniel into the house and got him to bed. Neither woman thought to worry about the precious quilt under his bloody arm and muddy boots.

Frances hurried off to get some hot water.

Mary Anna carefully moved Daniel's arm and used her scissors to cut away the crimson sleeve of his shirt. She studied the arrow still protruding out of his arm. "Tump, go tell Mrs. Gerald to bring a very sharp knife." The wide-eyed little boy sprinted for the kitchen.

As she worked, Mary Anna asked Daniel, "Where have you and Papa been? What happened?" Indistinguishable murmurs answered her.

Frances came in with the water and knife and gave a sharp glance at the arrow. She looked over to Mary Anna. "You know what to do?"

Mary Anna nodded and Frances stood by to help.

With swift movements, Mary Anna used the knife to cut off the tip of the arrow. She was grateful Daniel was unconscious as she struggled to pull the arrow through to the other side of his arm. Two yellow circles and a red line on the arrow would have told her who owned it had she known how the Comanche marked their arrows.

Fear helped her complete the grisly job of doctoring the man she loved. But would he survive the loss of blood and the infection that was bound to come?

"I'll go make willow bark tea," Frances offered. "Tump, you come with me and bring back the herbs your mama will need to put a poultice on that wound."

While their two little boys watched, huddled in silence, Mary Anna mopped Daniel's feverish brow with a cool rag and applied herbs to cleanse the wound and ease the pain. She eased sips of willow bark tea between his lips to take down the fever.

The fever seemed to make Daniel delirious. He sobbed and kept repeating how sorry he was. Mary Anna was shocked by the intensity of his painful words. She tried to shush him and calm him. "It's all right. It's all right. I'm here." What could have happened to wrench the heart of her brave, young husband?

Daniel heard her voice and understood what she was saying, but he couldn't make her understand what was wrong. He was certain Mary Anna would never love him again. He listened to her comfort, but as the medicine began to ease his pain, he began to drift. Back to the happy times when they weren't in this house on the raw Texas Frontier of Erath County.

He floated back to 1853 when he had first come to Texas, to Tennessee Colony in Anderson County.

ଈ

Daniel had just ridden in from his newly rented land to buy supplies at the mercantile store when he saw Mary Anna at the dry goods counter buying thread. She was the prettiest thing he'd ever seen. So tiny. So dainty, with her light brown hair piled up high to make her look taller. Her cornflower blue eyes were demure, and her manners genteel.

They hadn't been properly introduced, and even in the new settlement of Tennessee Colony in East Texas, a man couldn't expect a lady to talk with him. He wished she'd drop something so he could pick it up and then it would be all right to speak a little. Her voice wasn't as tiny as her frame, but it was pitched in a pleasing tone as she talked with the clerk. She was almost through with her purchases. She was going to leave.

Throwing away the restrictions of good manners, Daniel stepped forward and tipped his gray hat to her.

"Pardon me, ma'am, but I'd be honored if you'd accept a piece of peppermint."

She regarded him with those blue eyes, and her cheeks pinked at his brashness. She was about to say no thank you, but she saw he had almost the same color eyes as she did, and he was a very handsome man. He looked the picture of Southern gallantry standing there with his hand at the brim of his hat, waiting. "It really isn't proper, sir." But the light in her eyes told him she was going to accept his gift.

It wasn't that Mary Anna was improper. It was more that she was daring and resourceful. And as her eyes refused to pull away from the blue depths of his, she wondered why a simple offer of a piece of peppermint was making her heart beat so fast.

two

Tennessee Colony had the same unfinished look of the many other towns that were like fingers of civilization inching west across Texas in 1853.

Peter Garland, Mary Anna's father, was busy behind the desk of his hotel talking to a robust woman with hair the color of bad ginger.

"Please see that my bags git upstairs real fast," she said in the nasal tone of the unlettered.

"Yes, ma'am," he said without enthusiasm and signaled a small black boy to fetch the carpetbags.

His wife, Louisa, sidled up to him from the hot kitchen. "That daughter of yours is cooking like she's some kind of artist or something," she complained. "Go tell her to work faster and not try to be so fancy."

Peter, being a former military man and accustomed to war, was nevertheless irritated at the constant battles in his own household between his second wife and his pretty, sixteen-year-old daughter, Mary Anna.

Captain Peter Garland stood up straighter and said with quiet intensity, "Louisa, this has got to stop. I can't stand this constant yapping about Mary Anna." His eyes narrowed with anger and he warned, "If you're not careful, you'll be the one in that hot kitchen."

Louisa was totally unimpressed. "You think doing the laundry and cleaning this place is a lot of fun? Don't threaten me. Go talk to your daughter." She turned and walked away unhurriedly.

Having failed to quash his wife's agitation, Peter Garland

10

retreated to the sultry kitchen where his daughter turned out the food that brought people to his dining room.

Mary Anna was frying large steaks that had been pounded thin and tender, then dipped in a batter of flour, egg, and milk. The browned pieces of meat gave off a mouth-watering smell. It was their most popular dish, served with mounds of whipped, light-as-air potatoes and snowy white gravy with crisp bits of the crust hidden in each bite. When it came to cooking, his daughter *was* an artist. But how to bridge a compromise between wife and daughter?

Mary Anna wiped her hands on the apron around her tiny waist. "Did you want something, Papa?" she asked as she concentrated on thickening the gravy.

Peter's heart grew wobbly at the sight of his favorite child, the image of his dead wife. "No," he said, accepting total defeat at the sight of her, "Just be sure and save me a plate for dinner." He kissed her damp forehead and smiled.

When he returned to the desk, Louisa was waiting for her triumph. "Well?" she demanded. "Did you speak to her?"

"Yes, dear, I spoke to her," he said truthfully. Providence was on his side, for at that moment a young man walked in and strode up to the desk, ending the discussion.

"Good day to you, sir. Glad to have you with us. How long will you be staying?" Peter's greeting may have been a bit too friendly, but he was so glad to see his chance for ending his talk with his wife that he overplayed his hand.

"I'll be here a while," the young man said noncommittally. As he signed the register he commented, "Something sure smells good." He glanced toward the rough room that served as the dining room.

"Dinner is about ready. . .," Peter glanced at the name written on the register, "Mr. Thornton. My daughter is the best cook in Texas," he bragged, and then quickly looked around to see if Louisa had heard him. "By the time you take your bags upstairs and clean up a bit, she'll be serving."

"Thank you," Thornton replied and got the key to his room.

Peter watched him as he walked up the staircase. Thornton was a good-looking man, and Peter tried to assess his wealth by what he was wearing. Gray cowboy hat, expensive boots. No jewelry. It was a father's duty to check out all the new men in town. He had a marriageable daughter, and he wanted to pick out just the right man for his beloved Mary Anna. *Hmmmm, a maybe,* he decided.

❧

Daniel Thornton walked into the hotel room and set his leather bag on the floor at the end of the brass bed. He hung his hat on a wooden peg in the wall and poured some cool water from the china pitcher into the matching bowl. Carefully he rolled up the sleeves of his starched white shirt and leaned over the bowl, splashing the deliciously refreshing water on his tired, hot face. His stomach growled, reminding him it had been a long time since he'd had an unsatisfactory campfire breakfast on his newly leased farm land outside of town.

He checked his blue-black hair in the mirror and saw in its wavy reflection a man of twenty, but the eyes told of experiences older than that. For an instant he was startled to realize that his eyes were the same color as those of the comely young woman he had met at the mercantile store. Something about her had attracted him immediately. "Maybe it's the eyes," he grinned.

He was still tired from the hard labor of the past few days. He had cut timber and begun building a rude cabin. He planned to put in the crops as soon as that was done, but he hated sleeping on the ground.

When he had so adventurously left the Big House on the plantation in Mississippi to make his fortune in this new place called Texas, he'd never dreamed he'd miss his bed more than his family.

Even though this bed looked well-used, he couldn't resist stretching out on its colorful quilt. As the springs complained, he sighed and sank his head into the downy pillow. Absolutely anything was better than sleeping on the hard ground, using his saddle as a pillow. He dozed with a slight smile on his face, listening to the hallway sounds outside his room. With the window open he could hear the busyness of the town and smell that delicious food cooking somewhere down below him. It was a lot like being home again. He half expected the thin, black frame of his old mammy to come in, fussing at him about having his boots on the good bedspread. She had always been there for him through those growing up years, and he loved her as well as he did his own mother. He certainly knew her better.

His stomach registered a louder complaint, and the smell of the food propelled him downstairs to the dining room.

He saw her in an instant, placing hot food on the common table, bustling around like a mother at the head of a family. He tried to catch her eye, but she was too busy to notice.

He sat down next to a large woman with hair too red to believe and smiled his best smile at the comely young woman pouring hot coffee across the table.

She must have felt the smile for she looked up at him and stopped in mid-pouring, a blush from the heat already highlighting her soft skin. She returned his smile briefly and then dropped her eyes to finish her job.

He waited patiently for her to come to his side of the table and pour his coffee. She smelled of good food and sweet soap, and though her hands were very small, they looked strong and attractive as they poured the black liquid into his cup. He looked up into her face and saw those eyes again. Twin to his own. Something deep inside him reached for her, and he wondered if she felt it, too. There was nothing in her face to tell him. He had given her peppermint earlier, but now he felt he had given her his heart without knowing her. He tried to think of something to say.

"Your father says you're the best cook in Texas," he offered with a genuine smile. "I know it smells better than anything I've had since I left home." His voice had a pleasingly long Southern drawl.

"You're Irish, aren't you?" she countered.

"Irish by heritage, Southern by birth," he corrected her. "How can you tell?"

"First by your eyes and hair and second by your blarney."

"And you know because you're Irish, too. Right?"

"Yes." Her eyes danced with mischief. Never before had she felt so bold with a young man. First she had accepted candy from him, and now he was plying her with compliments and she was bantering with him like a coy debutante. This was not the way she had been brought up. And it felt wonderful.

"As one countryman to another, let me introduce myself." He rose and formally bowed. "I am Daniel Robert Thornton." He looked expectantly at her.

She curtsied and said, "I'm Mary Anna Garland, sir."

The people sitting around the table had all stopped eating and were gawking with mouths open at the little drama going on at their dinner table. The lady with the red hair had suspiciously watery eyes which she dabbed at with her napkin. "Ain't that sweet?" she said to her dinner partner. He looked at her as if she had lost her mind and took a large bite of a pickled egg.

Daniel took the hand Mary Anna extended and lightly kissed it. He wanted to put it in his shirt next to his heart. He wanted to wrap his arms around this extraordinary woman and carry her off to a castle. But he stood there holding her hand as if it were the crown jewels.

Mary Anna felt a little faint and realized it was from holding her breath. She exhaled and tried to break his gaze. She knew the entire room was watching, but she didn't care. There was electricity in the air, and it was coming from the touch of his hand on hers.

"Miss," whined an old geezer who had never known love, "could I have my coffee, please?"

The spell was broken, but Mary Anna walked inside a rainbow as she carried out her duties at the table. She knew Daniel had not taken his eyes off her, and the realization made her giddy.

Finally she retreated to the kitchen, taking in big gulps of air to clear her head. She had so often prayed for a fine Christian man with whom she could share her life. Had he walked in, just like that? *Lord, what's going on? Is this the man for me? I feel something strong about him. I'm excited and I feel silly.* She was standing at the stove stirring the vegetables as she prayed.

"What's wrong with you?" grumbled Louisa as she swished into the kitchen. She picked a small piece of the browned crust of an apple pie and studied her stepdaughter's glowing face for a second time.

Mary Anna was immediately on guard. "Nothing. I'm hot. Do you want plates for you and Pa?" she asked in an effort to redirect Louisa's thoughts.

"No, not yet. You know we always eat after all the guests are finished. Are you sure there's nothing wrong with you?" She stared hard at the young girl's face. Mary Anna was even more beautiful, her face radiating some sort of inner glow. Louisa took one last little pinch from the pie and left, still wondering what had gotten into the girl.

Daniel lingered as long as he dared at the table, but Miss Garland didn't come back. Reluctantly he paid the bill and left the hotel to take care of his business. There was no doubt in his mind where he would be taking supper that night.

Louisa watched the young man hang around the dining room, remembered the look on Mary Anna's face, and quickly put two and two together. What a stroke of luck! They were obviously taken with each other. All she had to do was make sure they spent some time together, and soon there would be a wedding. The problems of her life would be solved. Peter would concentrate on *her* once Mary Anna was married. She smiled broadly and began planning. *Sunday,* she decided. *There's a dinner on the ground after church.* Her smile broadened even more.

Louisa tried not to be jealous of the time her husband spent doting on Mary Anna. Louisa had seen the small locket with Mary Anna's mother's picture in it, and she was well aware that Mary Anna was a constant reminder to her husband of his dead wife. She hated that. She wanted to be his only love. Peter was kind and loving to her, but she never felt he loved her as much as he had his first wife.

She could make him love her that much or more if Mary Anna wasn't there to constantly remind him of his loss. The sooner she was gone, the sooner Louisa could begin to permanently erase the other woman from his life. Now that Mary Anna was of marriageable age, Louisa could find a husband for her. Louisa smiled in happiness. *This one looks like he could be the one.*

three

It was a perfect Sunday afternoon, and Louisa's plan was in full flower. Peter had invited Daniel to church and to the meal afterward, and he had eagerly accepted.

Now Daniel and Mary Anna sat underneath the umbrella of green leaves swishing the air beneath them like a thousand tiny servants moving fans to cool them.

Daniel groaned appreciatively and tried to ease his long frame into a more comfortable position on the patchwork quilt. "That's the best apple pie I've ever had." He washed the last of it down with a gulp of cold lemonade.

His heart rate had steadied since its first wild gallop at the sight of her at church. He had endured the eternal sermon and sung the hymns with a fair baritone, and when it had come time to pray, had he still believed that God was personally involved in his life, he would have had only one prayer—that she would love him as much as he loved her. And then it was time for the meal.

The Thorntons had invited Daniel to sit with them, but they couldn't all sit on the same blanket, so he and Mary Anna had a blanket to themselves now that her younger brothers and sisters had run off to play.

Mary Anna's voice was as clear and sweet sounding as water to a thirsty man. "How long has it been since you've been home?" She was tidying up, putting things in the big hamper.

"About a year." He tipped the soft brim of his hat up a little higher on his forehead and watched her.

"Don't you miss your family terribly?"

"Yes. But coming out west was something I had to do." He

17

smiled an embarrassed smile. "I needed to make some money of my own. I got tired of being obliged to my father." Idly he picked a piece of grass to chew on. "Pretty country, Texas."

She leaned against the big shady old oak and laughed softly. "I remember the day we crossed the border into Texas. It took us a month to come from Tennessee. There were thirty covered wagons in our train, but they were so heavily loaded that all the older children had to walk. I was twelve. Then one day someone shouted, 'We made it! This here is Texas!' I was so disappointed. It looked just like all the country we'd covered. I couldn't understand how they knew we were in Texas. All I wanted to do was to stop walking and sit."

Daniel laughed delightedly. "So you walked to Texas! I walked a lot of the way from Mississippi. We have a lot in common." His eyes sparkled with an intimacy that stirred Mary Anna's senses in a most disturbing way.

She smiled at his enjoyment of her story and took in the handsome face so open before her. A crowd of people was busy eating and laughing all around them, but they were in a private world of their own.

"Some day," he told her, "I'm going to own so many horses and cows that I'll be able to ride from my table to my bed if I've a mind to."

"Richer than your father," she laughed.

"Texas is the land of milk and honey, so the tale goes." His smile was pragmatic. "So far all I've seen is a lot of milk, but the time will come." He left the thought full of promise and adventure, and she could feel his unrestrained excitement. "I want to build my own kingdom. There's so much land out there just waiting to be used. Why, a man could have a ranch of thousands and thousands of acres." He gave a crooked grin. "Maybe I'm just trying to do better than my father. I want him to be proud of me."

Mary Anna felt her heart quicken at the thought of what this man planned to accomplish. It matched her own dreams of being her own person. She wrinkled her forehead in puzzlement. "But why have you stopped to farm in Tennessee Colony if you plan to go farther west?"

"I'm a greenhorn when it comes to pioneering. I've been learning all the things I'll need to know when there's no one around to ask." He leaned forward in his earnestness. "I need to know how to build a cabin, how to plant crops, and which ones I'll need. I'm already a good shot, but I don't know how to skin deer or buffalo. There's an awful lot to learn," he conceded. "And I'll need money."

Mary Anna wanted to memorize the picture of this tall, well-muscled man. His sun-bronzed face was young and strong, full of dreams and plans. With his hat tipped back, a small band of skin that had been shaded from the Texas sun was exposed, and the sight of that pale streak below his hairline seemed a most intimate sight. She wanted to reach out and stroke the well-defined chin, the strong jawline, the mobile mouth. It was on his mouth that her eyes lingered. "How long will you stay here?"

His eyes met hers. "A while. 'Til I make enough money to keep going. I want to keep moving west. There are millions of acres just waiting to be tamed." His face hardened. "Now that the murdering Comanches have been taken care of, it should be safe for a man to make his fortune."

"But we have reports all the time that there are still bands of them wandering wherever they please," she contradicted him. Hatred marbleized his face.

"It won't be too long 'til the government has them all locked up where they belong. Reservation life is the best thing for them. It keeps us peaceful people safe."

The injustice of his statement hit Mary Anna like a hammer. She took a deep breath and plunged in, fearless to speak her mind. "They were here long before us. We're the intruders.

And they're only fighting to protect what rightfully belongs to them." Her quick temper and sharp tongue had earned her a reputation of some note in the community.

Daniel's face darkened with suppressed rage. "There's enough land for everybody. No need to be killing white people just so they can protect land they're wasting. They don't do anything but ride around all over it."

Mary Anna liked this young man, and as his rage increased, hers lessened. She quietly asked, "What happened to make you hate the Indians so much?"

Daniel's teeth ground together tightly. "When my grandfather was clearing his land in Virginia, the Indians captured him. They tortured him before they took his scalp for the tent pole. I was the one who found him." The horror of that day was reflected in the haunted eyes that stared out into the far-too-recent past. "'Course my father killed two of them later for revenge, but that didn't erase what they did to Grandpa."

Mary Anna sat paralyzed with the horror of the story and the depths of bitterness revealed by a man she had admired from the moment she had first seen him.

"Are you shocked?" At the dumb nodding of her head, he went on defiantly. "You don't live in the real world here, Miss Garland. Out there it's just you against everything else, and I do mean everything." He pulled the brim of his hat down until it shaded his eyes—and perhaps some of his feelings. "If it makes you feel any better, I have no intention of killing any more Indians for my Grandpa. That's over and done. But if I ever had to kill to protect myself or my loved ones, I'd never stop to think about it. That rich land out there was made for ranching and farming, and I intend to work for my fair share. No murdering savages are going to keep me from earning it."

A thousand words of protest rushed to Mary Anna's lips, but the firm set of Daniel's jaw and the resolute look in his eyes broke her desperate desire to argue with him.

The goldenness of the day was tarnished. The conversations that had flowed so freely were now swollen into hidden cataracts that tossed their struggling participants into dangerous areas.

Daniel and Mary Anna limped through the rest of their time together, pretending nothing had happened, and the farewell that they bade when he walked her home was equally strained.

Mary Anna slammed the door to the bedroom she shared with her three younger half-sisters and threw herself across the bed, heartsick with her new knowledge. How could she possibly respect a man with so large a blind spot and so much hatred in his heart?

Almost everyone she knew had been troubled by the Indians. Many had had relatives killed by them, too.

No one had forgotten the raid on Fort Parker only thirteen years earlier and the kidnapping of Cynthia Ann, her brother, and several other whites by the Comanche. Fort Parker was only fifty miles southwest of Tennessee Colony. No one had found or accounted for Cynthia Ann and her brother yet. The grisly affair was still retold when people wanted to cite the cruelty of the Indians. It was rumored that Cynthia Ann was living with an Indian man and riding with him as he raided with his band of warriors, killing more whites and stealing their horses. Mothers warned disobedient children of "what happened to Cynthia Ann."

But Mary Anna had a strong sense of fair play that caused her to question the white man's right to simply take land away from anyone. The contradictory nature of her feelings made her wish sometimes that her family had never left Tennessee.

She tried to recapture the goodness of the time she and Daniel had spent together before his awful revelation of his feelings. The pleasant memories wouldn't come.

That night as she tossed and turned in her bed, she realized that she could never share her life with a man who had such hatred burning in him. She prayed her nightly prayers, adding, *And Lord, would you please change his heart. He seems like a good man. Someone I could love. Melt the hatred and clear out the anger.*

She knew the Lord could do this, but would He? She would wait to see if the Lord would give her any signs of change in Daniel's heart. Meanwhile, she would try to keep her distance. She was heart-sick at the sudden demise of her dream.

At meal times when Daniel came into the hotel, she stayed in the kitchen as much as possible. And when she served the table, she did it quickly and without friendly conversation. She was civil to Daniel at church, but distant and formal.

It was fairly easy to dismiss him socially, but it was almost impossible to banish him completely from her thoughts. He had been so gallant, so easy to talk with, so handsome.

She smiled ruefully as she remembered it had been the easy talking that had caused the problem. She longed to see him, but the naked hatred she had seen in his face frightened her. There was no reason to allow him into her life. It just couldn't work. Mr. Daniel Thornton could go west to follow his dream. She hoped it would be very soon.

☙

Peter Garland knew something was very wrong with his girl, but he hadn't been sharp enough to see it, so Louisa told him what she thought had happened. "It's obvious they've had some sort of quarrel. I can't understand what it could be about, though. They hardly know one another."

So he waited until he could be alone with Mary Anna in the kitchen.

"Darlin'," he said softly. "I can see things have not gone right between you and young Mr. Thornton. What happened?"

The pent-up tears broke over the levee Mary Anna had carefully constructed around her heart, and she wept all over the front of her father's freshly pressed shirt, pouring out her sad story. He held her and patted her shoulder awkwardly, nodding his head and trying to make sense out of the tear-garbled words. When he was fairly sure he understood the problem, he had no answer for it, so he held her and let her cry.

"And every time I turn around he's there," she finished with a wail.

Ah, there was something he might be able to do after all. "They're needing a school teacher. He wouldn't be coming to the school bothering you. Maybe you should work there until he's gone. We can get along here without you for a while." It was the only solution Peter could think of on the spur of the moment, and he knew there would be a heavy price to pay when Louisa learned he had let his daughter out of the kitchen. Boldly he went with Mary Anna down to the mayor's store to apply for the job.

Mary Anna had no doubt she could teach school. She had read every book she could get her hands on and was good in math. With the help of books and maps and a chalkboard, she could do a good job. She was concerned that there wasn't a schoolhouse yet, but in her haste to get away from the handsome Mr. Thornton, she accepted the monthly salary of fifteen dollars and walked to the brush arbor where logs were split and pegged and set in rows.

It was worse than disheartening that the books were old and ragged and few. There were a few broken slates and pieces of chalk. But the worst was yet to come.

Mary Anna had students ranging from the first to the ninth grades. Sometimes there was one pupil in each grade, sometimes there were several. But the older boys were twice as big as she was, and she was hard put to make them behave. They kept nudging one another and whispering and smiling at her. It took all her skills to get through the morning as the sun and the temperature climbed higher and the shade from the arbor got smaller. This wasn't what she'd had in mind when she'd accepted the job, but it was hers and she wasn't a quitter.

At least her new job kept her from seeing Daniel except occasionally at church. She continued to pray for him—mostly that he would go away because she couldn't imagine even the Lord melting his hatred away quickly.

The week dragged to a limp conclusion, and when Mary Anna awakened Saturday, she smiled with relief. This was one of the busiest days at the hotel, and she could stay home and would only have to keep up with the youngest of the children. The rest would be working in the hotel.

Louisa had raged when she'd learned that Peter had excused Mary Anna from working at the hotel, but to make peace, Mary Anna had agreed to do the family wash and baking.

She was in the middle of baking the bread while the wash soaked in the big black pot out in the yard when she heard someone approaching the cabin. She wiped her hands on her apron and covered up the rising dough with a towel. By the time the knock sounded, she was ready to answer the door.

He was standing in the open door, silhouetted by the brightness of the sun. Her heart leaped at the sight of him, yet was instantly on guard. Her hands trembled, and she gathered up her apron to hide them.

"My father isn't here."

Daniel stepped inside and took off his hat. His blue eyes bore into hers as though to hypnotize her. "You know I didn't come to see your father." He stood quietly, waiting for her to say something.

She saw the loneliness and hurt in his eyes. Unbidden love flooded her heart and made it ache. Dazedly she motioned him to come in. She was having a hard time breathing, and the cabin seemed to be shrinking.

"You knew I'd come," he said softly.

"Yes," and suddenly she did know it.

"I've missed you."

She wasn't ready to concede that she had missed him, too.

He went on in his soft southern drawl. "You were upset after I told you about my grandpa."

"No," she corrected him, "I was upset after you told me how you feel about Indians."

He walked away from her, pausing before the unlit fireplace with his back to her. Mary Anna followed and stood beside her mother's rocking chair, her hand resting on the carved headrest so she wouldn't reach out to him.

With his back still turned, Daniel began to speak. "I don't expect you to understand everything about me or to approve of it." He turned around slowly, his face pleading for a fair hearing. Electricity raced between them, pushing them together and pulling them apart. Mary Anna felt the intensity of his words resonate in her heart.

Daniel stepped forward and put his hand on hers. The rocking chair moved slightly with the added weight.

"No matter what has come between us, I know only one thing. From the moment I saw you in that store, I knew you were special. Even though you're so tiny, you carried yourself with such assurance. I liked the way your chin tipped up, almost defiantly, just the way it is now."

She leveled her head and tried desperately not to be aware of the warm hand holding hers captive.

"When we sat on the quilt at the picnic, I wanted to tell you everything about myself from the time I was born until that day." He raised her chin up with his other hand to look into her eyes. "I even wanted you to know the bad things about me. Somehow I knew you'd understand."

She cried out, "But I don't understand."

"I know that now, but you will. . .eventually."

His face was coming nearer her own, eyes closing and mouth parting. Her arms rose of their own accord to clasp around his neck. His mouth gently touched hers, exploring, softly pressing and releasing, and coming back again. An unnamed longing filled her and spilled out into the kiss that she was now returning with shameless abandon.

His voice rasped words against her mouth. "Come with me, Mary Anna. Marry me and come with me on my great adventure. I don't ever want to be without you again as long as I live." As though to force the answer he wanted from her, he intensified his mouth's searching of hers. "I love you."

All her reservations, all her doubts about him melted in the intense heat of their embrace. "Yes, Daniel, yes." Her entire being reached for him and fused them into one as she said, "I love you, too."

"We'll build an empire together. We'll have sons and daughters and build a new world. You'll be my queen in the wilderness we'll tame together."

"Sounds to me like you have some mighty big plans," Peter's big voice boomed into their private world.

Daniel kept his arm around Mary Anna's waist possessively as he faced Peter, calm and assured. "Yes, Mr. Garland. I want Mary Anna to marry me and come west. I'm asking for your blessing."

Peter's face was stern as he walked toward Daniel. "Before I give you my beloved daughter, I need to know some things." He looked levelly into the waiting blue eyes. "Will you always care for her and never, ever mistreat her?"

Daniel's yes was firm.

"I already heard you say you loved each other, but love is a funny thing. It comes and goes in a marriage. Can you be best friends?"

Daniel laughed. "I'm counting on that, sir."

Peter's eyes dimmed with unshed tears. "He's taking you west, child. Are you sure?"

Unflinchingly she answered, "Yes, Pa." Her face gave off the luminous glow of new love.

"Then I guess we're having us a wedding," Peter said with as much joy as he could muster. "Welcome to the family, son," he said to Daniel as he stuck out his hand.

When Mary Anna went to bed that night, she couldn't sleep for the excitement and joy that raced through her. Long after her stepsisters had fallen asleep, she lay thinking of what had happened so suddenly. But in the darkness, she couldn't ignore the one niggling doubt that kept poking a pin into her happiness.

Lord, there isn't any sign that Daniel has changed his mind about the Indians. But I love him so much, and when he touched me, I thought I would melt like a candle in the wind. I can't live without him, Lord, so I'm assuming that You will change him as time goes by. Help me to soften his heart. I know he will change once we're married. I just know he will change. He's a good man. And thank You for bringing him into my life. Thank You. She fell asleep with those words on her lips.

❧

In the weeks that followed, plans for Mary Anna and Daniel's wedding and their life together were made. They wouldn't be going west right away, a relief for Mary Anna and her father. She wanted adventure, but the Lord had given her love and security for a while.

Mary Anna had a new dress for her wedding. She had sent away for the material, and Louisa had happily made it from a picture in the catalog. It was simple, but she looked beautiful in the pale, blue-green material that made her eyes look even bluer. A perky straw hat trimmed with lace sat at a jaunty angle on her pompadour hairdo, making her look older than her sixteen years.

Daniel was the best-looking groom the town had ever seen. His white shirt had extra starch that made it rattle as he bent his elbows. His boots were shined until he could see himself in the glowing toes, and he had gotten a new suit with an appropriate tie. His blue-black hair was combed just so, and the shadow over his mouth where he was growing his mustache was soft and pleasing.

The ceremony was simple. Mary Anna's family and most of the town joined the celebration, and the small church was hard pressed to hold everyone. It was the hottest July they'd ever had, and everyone felt the effects of the stifling heat in the small building.

The wedding supper was held at the hotel's dining room, and a fiddle and harmonica provided music for dancing in the lobby.

It was late when the newly married couple climbed into a borrowed carriage and rode out to the newly finished cabin on Daniel's rented land.

"We're on our way home," Mary Anna said happily.

Daniel looked up at the moon hanging in the hazy heavens. "Yes, we are." And he kissed his wife gently under the watchful eyes of a million stars.

four

During the four years they lived out on the farm, Daniel and Mary Anna forged their marriage as well as the land. Forged was a good term for it, for Daniel learned that his lovely bride had the temper of a volcano. But her explosions were usually short-lived, and the making up was wonderful.

With great pride Mary Anna presented Daniel a son, Columbus Erastus, two years after they were married. Life wasn't so hard. The small family accumulated and made what they needed and prepared for the day when they would pack up and head west. During the winter of 1856, they made their final plans. They would have to leave well ahead of the spring rains that flooded the Trinity and Brazos Rivers.

Mary Anna spoke to her father about the impending trip.

"It's so exciting, Pa. We'll be like a ship out on the ocean."

Peter frowned. "I'd feel better if you were traveling in a wagon train. It'd be so much safer."

"Oh, Pa, where we're going there aren't any Indians." She put a cup of coffee in front of him and added three lumps of sugar, the way he liked it.

He gazed out the cabin window at the neat rows of dirt waiting for spring seed. Daniel was in the shed feeding the cow. "All the bad things out there aren't red." He sighed, knowing the ugliness of the world and wanting to shield his daughter.

She gave the toddling Columbus a helping hand as he tried to walk from his little chair to his grandfather. Having made it, he pulled at Peter's pants leg, trying to get into his lap. "I'm going to miss you, son," he told the blond-haired boy softly. His words were meant for Mary Anna, too.

But the day arrived when there was no time to delay. The wagon was loaded with their household goods, and the chicken coop was strapped on. Every inch of space in the wagon was accounted for, and the family's cattle and horses were herded together.

After the loading, both families joined together for prayer. Peter led them. "Father, these young people are going off to build a new life for themselves, and we ask You to be with them all the way. Keep them safe, give them wisdom and courage. But most of all, Lord, let them always know that You are there with them, no matter what. Amen."

Daniel hoped that the prayer would be effective, though he couldn't believe God would intervene in his family's life. He felt the enormous weight of keeping his little family safe, and it was a somber man who led his family away from the safety of Tennessee Colony toward the dream he had to follow.

It was still bitterly cold, and the breath of both animals and people plumed in the air. Hastily the good-byes were said. It was too hard to prolong the parting.

But as they began their journey with Daniel astride his favorite horse and Mary Anna driving the wagon with Columbus tucked behind her, Mary Anna's heart soared. *It is going to happen. Now. Today. The beginning of the dream starts now.*

&

After the noon stop, Daniel tied his horse behind the wagon and climbed up beside Mary Anna.

"Westward we go," she said excitedly. "How far? Have you decided?"

"I've heard that the foothills of the Palo Pinto Mountains are so rich with grass that cattle spring up out of the ground by themselves just to eat it," he grinned.

"We talked of stopping between the Brazos and the Trinity. You want to go farther?"

His eyes focused on the horizon. "I have this scene in my

mind, dreamed it several times." Confidently he added, "I'll know it when I see it." He looked at her furrowed brow. "Don't worry. We're not on our way to the Pacific Ocean." He saw her relax a little and couldn't resist teasing. "Just to the Rocky Mountains."

"Thank goodness I didn't marry a man with wandering feet," she said wryly.

The days became as rhythmic as the swaying of the wagon, and a familiar pattern developed. Mary Anna felt safe with Daniel beside her. There was time to plan and dream and play with Columbus. He was a bit of a handful and needed constant supervision to keep him out of the things two-year-olds need to explore.

The only time Mary Anna was uneasy was when Daniel rode off to scout up ahead. The sudden absence of her husband left her alert and acutely aware of her sole responsibility for the baby. She had her cap and ball rifle beside her, and she knew how to use it. But they had not seen a single soul since they'd left Tennessee Colony. With Daniel gone, she had the eerie feeling she and the baby were the last two people on the entire earth.

As the hours passed, that feeling eased and she was able to enjoy the countryside. Daniel was up ahead, herding the stock and breaking the trail. She knew they'd be stopping soon to make camp for the night. It was easy to follow the wide swath of crushed grass, and the broken blades gave off a pungent perfume. It was like floating on a sweet, crackling river. The rolling hills took her up and down, always leading to the man she loved.

It had been hard leaving her family. Even Louisa had gotten misty-eyed as they'd embraced in farewell. Mary Anna wasn't sure exactly what had happened between them, but Louisa had gone from being a hard woman to treating Mary Anna kindly when Daniel proposed. "I guess it had something to do with jealousy," Mary Anna told Daniel. "Whatever the reason, I'm grateful. I only wish she had been this loving with me before."

When Mary Anna had gone into labor with Columbus, Louisa had helped her deliver the child. Mary Anna smiled, remembering the first cries from that tiny, squirming bundle. Life had been wonderful during these first four years. Now she was twenty years old with a husband and a child, and she was off on a wondrous journey to a new home.

They forded the Trinity River with only a little difficulty, and the Brazos with heady success. "The Lord is surely taking care of us, Daniel," she said as the back wheels of the wagon hit solid ground.

He didn't respond. Daniel's faith in God being personally involved in his life had ended the day he had found his grandfather's mutilated body. So every time Mary Anna spoke of God, he kept quiet.

They made night camp and had a simple hot supper. Daniel poured himself another cup of coffee as Mary Anna tucked Columbus into the wagon bed, then they sat down together by the fire.

"Just look at those stars. Seems a man could almost reach up and pick one," he said.

"And what would you do with a star?" she teased him.

"Why, I'd give it to my best girl." The firelight revealed his love for her in his big blue eyes.

"I believe that some day you will do just that."

Daniel rose and tossed the remains of his coffee on the fire, then carefully banked it. There was no need for more words as they prepared to settle down in the wagon. There would be another night of love out in the grassy sea with only the stars and the moon as observers.

৯৯

Daniel and Mary Anna had been on the trail for almost three weeks, and still they hadn't met anyone.

"I thought we'd at least see some Indians or bandits or some-body," she said thoughtfully.

"Worried?"

"No."

"Scared?"

"A little," she admitted. She lifted her chin and looked steadily at him. "I believe this is what the Lord wants us to do, and He's led us this far safely. I have a strong, smart husband to take care of me, too. So it's okay for me to be a little scared." She laughed, and then looked at him carefully. "Aren't you just a little scared?"

"Not yet. We haven't had anything to be scared of." He looked serious. "Life out here won't be easy, and I know the scary times will come. Let's don't borrow from tomorrow."

The next day Daniel was out ahead, scouting. Mary Anna's eyes scanned the horizon for him. The dried grass was still high from last summer, and there was a promise of spring in the air. Mary Anna was breathing hard with excitement. Daniel was surely going to decide today. Then she saw a rider gallop-ing toward her at full speed. He was waving his hat in the air and shouting.

"We're here! Hurry those oxen along. We're home!"

They topped a small rise. A good-sized spring bubbled and ran off to the right, making a small stream of clear water. A large stand of timber forested the rise behind it like dark green velvet drapery. The wind rubbed the wintery blades of grass together, creating a swishing, whispering symphony that wel-comed them to the land of their dreams.

Mary Anna froze with the awesome beauty before her. She could barely whisper, "Daniel, it's perfect."

They stood, arms around each other, looking at the land the Palo Pinto Mountains cradled at their feet.

Mary Anna swept Columbus up out of the wagon. "Look, baby. It's our new home. Your new home." She turned her face up to her husband, radiant with joy, and felt his finger trace one of the tears streaming down her face.

"I haven't seen you cry since you showed me Columbus." His face was soft with love.

"Some people cry when they're sad. I cry only when I'm happy."

"Then I hope there will be many tears for you here." He sighed contentedly and helped Mary Anna and the baby back into the wagon for the short ride down to the spring.

When they reached the water, they held hands and Mary Anna prayed. "Lord, we thank You for the safe trip here. We thank You for this beautiful country. We ask that You would bless the labors of our hands and help us to be worthy of all these blessings. Amen."

Mary Anna's eyes swept the vast countryside. "When we decided to come out here, I was sure I wanted to. Then when we got started, I wondered if we'd done the right thing." She chuckled. "Sort of reminded me of the Bible story of Peter stepping out of the boat in faith and trying to walk to Jesus on the water." She turned to Daniel with earnest eyes. "If we keep our eyes on the Lord, we won't sink," she said with conviction. Daniel nodded his head more in admiration of her faith than belief in her words.

That night, Mary Anna carefully noted in her journal that her family settled in Dripping Springs on February 20, 1857.

Daniel woke the next morning and started marking the outside walls of the cabin before Mary Anna had stirred up the fire and made the coffee.

"You'll be worn out before I get the bacon fried," she teased.

"You just get that meal made and then we'll build our castle."

"Castle?" she grinned.

He scuffed his toe in the dirt and looked sheepishly at her. "Well, maybe it will feel like a castle after living in the wagon for so long."

Over the next weeks, Daniel cut the trees and used the oxen

to drag and lift the logs. It was bitterly cold, and the animals' body heat came off in plumes of steam.

After days of helping Daniel where she could and going to the icy river to make caulking from clay, mud, and grass, Mary Anna longed for the house to be built quickly, but she held her tongue around Daniel. They were both so exhausted by the time they had eaten supper that they cuddled up with Columbus between them and slept the sleep of the overly tired.

Daniel had marked off a tiny, one-room cabin. Constructing it was backbreaking work in the bitter cold. "I know it's small," he apologized, "but it's strong. We'll add on as we can."

They covered the roof with split shingles and made a shelf outside the door with a round hole in it for a wash bowl. Mary Anna hugged Daniel hard when she saw he had taken the time to make this extra nicety.

Both their hands were raw and blistered from the hard labor—especially Mary Anna's. She was vain about her looks, and building a cabin in the middle of the frontier in late February was not a lady-like job. But she gritted her teeth and tried to work as hard as Daniel. Pride was another of her faults, but she wasn't about to let Daniel think he had married a weak, helpless woman. Each night she put salve on her wounded hands, as well as on his.

"I was thinking we'll probably be able to move everything into the cabin tomorrow," he said as they sat by the supper fire. Mary Anna was busy doctoring his hands. He looked at her with great love. "I know this hasn't been as much fun as when we all got together and raised a cabin in a day. And there's no one around to have a party with afterwards. I want you to know I'm proud of all your hard work and I love you all the more for it."

Her eyes met his. "I love you with all my heart, and I'm not one bit sorry we're here." She gave a tiny smile. "It is too bad about not having the people here for a party. I would love to show off our lovely new home." He moved closer to her and lifted her chin with the tip of his finger, moving her mouth to his. The kiss was long and deep and told both of them the things their hearts couldn't say out loud.

≈

The next day, Daniel was wet with hard labor and panting from hefting up the thick door and setting it in place. He stepped back to look at the snug little cabin. "Good job, don't you think?" he asked proudly.

"I certainly do." Then Mary Anna cocked her head to the side and her eyes crinkled with mischief. "I think the servants quarters should be over there, and I'll need a summer kitchen, and let's see, don't forget—"

Daniel grabbed her, threw her over his shoulder, and started walking toward the small river while she screamed, "Don't do it, Daniel, I'm warning you, don't do it!" He laughed loudly as he dumped her into the cold water, but she had hooked her hand tightly into the top of his pants, and he lost his balance, following her into the stream.

"Not my hat! Save my hat!" he shouted and threw it toward the bank.

The cold water was shocking, but it felt good to both of them and they made good use of the short time they stayed there. The cool air made them towel off quickly and change into dry clothing. Daniel was pulling on another pair of boots as he said, "I hadn't planned on a bath today." He added, "You're lucky you didn't get my hat wet, or you'd be a drowned kitten right now."

"That'll teach you to mess around with an Irish girl," Mary Anna said smugly as she struggled with her dry petticoats. Little Columbus looked up in wonder at his playful parents.

"Son," Daniel said with mock sadness, "don't ever marry an Irish girl. All they'll bring you is trouble."

"And the strongest loving you'll ever have in your lifetime," Mary Anna added as she snuggled up against his broad chest.

five

It was dawn, and Mary Anna rested her head against the side of the cow she was milking. Columbus was happily playing inside the little playpen Daniel had built to contain him while Mary Anna did her chores in the cow lot. If she turned her head, she could see Daniel plowing with the oxen. He was using a forked tree for a plow fastened to the double tree from the wagon. It was clumsy, but effective.

Steady spurts of warm milk foamed the bucket, and tiny wisps of steam feathered the crispness of the late winter air. Mary Anna smiled as little Columbus happily chirped away. When the babbling stopped, she instinctively looked up. Her heart stopped. Three Indian braves were standing beside her child.

The sheer terror of the moment passed as she tried to take stock of the situation. The men were not holding weapons, but knives were strapped against their waists. They were dressed in an odd assortment of white man's clothing.

Their faces bore no anger, rather a combination of serenity and pride. Mary Anna's cap and ball rifle was leaning against the cow pen's wall, out of her reach. Daniel was out in the fields. What could they want? If only they would move away from Columbus! She had to distract them from the child. Unsteadily she rose from the milking stool and with deliberate calmness walked toward them.

Hoping her smile looked natural, she took measured steps to the playpen. She nodded politely to the stone-faced men while reaching in and taking the baby in her arms.

"Good day." She looked straight into the eyes of the man she had singled out as the leader, fearlessly holding the look until he spoke.

He looked her over deliberately, stared at the child, and then at the cow. When he again looked at her, he spoke with unconcerned insolence. "You are small."

Was this a challenge? What chance did she have against three men, even if she had been as tall as they? With unhurried coolness she answered. "Yes, I am small in body, but my heart is as large as these lands."

"Yes," he agreed. "It must be for one woman and one man to come so far from their people."

So he knew how many they were and that they were alone. Did he also know how far away Daniel was? Where were the Indians' horses? The thought that there might be many more men holding their horses in the trees around the stream filled her with terror.

To fight the fear, she challenged them, praying she wouldn't make them angry. "What do you want?" Her voice was steady. She waited to see anger, but instead saw the tiniest glimmer of amusement.

"You have a sharp tongue. You make good Indian wife." He ignored her question. With a slow movement of his hand he reached up and touched the blond ringlets of Columbus' head. "Pretty baby."

"A good baby, like his father." She willed herself not to pull back from the frightening hand.

It came back down slowly. "You have meat to give." It was a statement of fact.

Daniel's voice answered the question from behind her. "Yes, we have meat. Come with me to the cabin." He was carrying his rifle loosely in his hand, and he motioned toward the little home with it.

The warrior made a sound of assent and walked toward the cabin. He waited with his two companions outside the door as Mary Anna entered with Daniel.

"Get that turkey you smoked," Daniel ordered quietly.

Mary Anna got the wrapped poultry and gave it to him. She watched from the door as Daniel handed it to the silent men. They turned and walked toward the stand of trees by the stream, and Daniel came back inside.

Daniel continued to watch the men as they strode into the woods. Venomously he spat out, "How dare they come walking in here demanding meat!"

His anger shocked Mary Anna out of her fear, and her face became red with unspent anger. Shaking, she put Columbus down on the floor, and then collapsed beside him.

"He touched the baby! I thought I'd die when he touched the baby!"

Daniel's face was twisted in rage. "They're probably renegades from the reservation."

He lost sight of the men and put the gun in its place over the fireplace. He was trembling with anger. The men had caught him off guard, and he had chosen a path of peace rather than standing and fighting them. He was ashamed of his lack of courage. He tried to justify his actions to himself and his wife. "Ugly looking things, weren't they? Pitiful. No horses, so they can't hunt. I felt kind of sorry for them." He avoided looking at Mary Anna.

Now that she was safe, Mary Anna thought of the men differently. She thought they were very regal. Haughty, in spite of their odd clothing. "Do you think they would have harmed us?"

"Yes, if they hadn't known I was nearby—and if they hadn't gotten something to eat. There's a reservation down on the Brazos that they're supposed to stay on, but some of them still run around. Some escape. Don't ever take any chances with them. They'd kill you in a minute if it suited them. I don't want to get in a fight, but I'd never let them hurt you or the baby."

Cautiously she speculated. "Maybe they were just hungry, but don't worry, I won't ever take any chances. Daniel, I couldn't get to the gun. It was propped on the wall away from me. Oh, how could I have been so stupid! From now on I'm taking the pistol with me in my apron pocket."

"Good idea. I'll leave my rifle here with you and get the one from the cow pen." He looked at her sternly. "You know now what we're up against. Don't ever be unprepared." Then he walked over to her and hugged her hard.

She lightly laughed. "Is it all right if I'm scared now?"

He gave her a small grin. "It's all right. It's all over. You did well out there." He shook his head. "You didn't look scared to me. You're some kind of woman, Mary Anna Thornton." There was pride in his voice and his step was brisk as he went out to continue his plowing.

Mary Anna hurried out to retrieve the milk bucket. It was a very fast trip.

Once she was safely back in the cabin, she gathered Columbus in her arms and sat in her mother's rocking chair, humming and cuddling him. The picture of the Indian man's dark hand touching the tow-headed boy's ringlets wouldn't go away. She had no idea what the man had been thinking, but she had heard such horrible tales of scalps on tent poles and of children taken and never heard of again that she began to pray. "Thank You, God, thank You."

Columbus enjoyed her loving for a while, then grew restless to be down playing with his wooden toys on the hard dirt floor.

With a calmer heart, Mary Anna began the noon meal. There was plenty of wild game, and she made a thick soup with some venison.

Before long there would be berries of all sorts, and her vegetable garden would come in, but they were running low on flour. She couldn't ask Daniel to make the twelve-hour trip to Stephenville for that. But what would she do if she ran out of flour? They had to have bread.

She worried the problem around in her head as she finished making dinner. It was as she was buttering a large slice of bread that a possible solution occurred to her. Using one of her large crocks, she set some of the skimmed milk close to the fire and covered it. When Daniel came in, she didn't mention her idea.

"Hmm, it smells good in here." Daniel had washed up and sat at the table with a grin on his face. The plowing had worked off the last of his anger. "It surely was a good day when I saw you in that store. Never have I been sorry I married the best cook in Anderson County."

Mary Anna deliberately pressed close to him and challenged, "So you married me only because I was a good cook?"

He returned her wide smile. "Well, now I know there's more to marriage than good cooking."

&

The next morning, after she had done her outside chores, Mary Anna took the curdling milk from beside the fire and wrapped it in a cloth to drain off the liquid. She squeezed and pressed until the curds were dry and then rubbed in a little salt. Then she hung it up close to the fire again to completely dry the curds.

There was a lot to do, but Mary Anna had worked out a logical way to accomplish all the work necessary to feed and clothe her family between taking care of Columbus.

She especially enjoyed this time of year when the earth was waking up and shaking all living things out of its covers. Noisy birds filled the air, and fragile spring flowers peeked from under warm patches of earth. Everything smelled so fresh and new and promising. She did as much of her work outdoors as she could, but the rifle was never far from her hand. She had learned her lesson about that carelessness.

She took down the cottage cheese from the fireplace and

tested its dryness. It crumbed nicely. With her fingers she made the curds even smaller and put them out in the sun to dry a little more. Finally she ground the whole batch into a semblance of flour. She made bread with it and put it in the dutch oven in the coals. It wasn't long until it smelled like bread.

When Daniel came in for his noon meal, she sliced up the fresh, hot bread and served it to him without comment.

Carefully she watched his first bite. "What did you do to the bread?" he asked.

"Isn't it all right?" she asked innocently.

"It tastes good, just different. More like sourdough biscuits or something."

With great pride she told him of her idea.

"It worked, but I think I'll plan to make a run for supplies," Daniel said. "I noticed the coffee was getting a little low, and I don't want to think what you might do if we run out of coffee!"

They both put up a brave front when the supply trip was mentioned. Now that they knew Indians were in the area, they dared not leave their place unprotected. Mary Anna would have to stay alone while Daniel got the things they needed.

That night in bed, Daniel confronted her. "Will you be all right?"

"Of course," she said brightly.

He leaned over and laid his head on her pillow. "It'd be all right if you used up some of your scared feelings." He pulled her into his arms. "I'll do everything I can to make it easier for you and to make you safe."

"I know." She looked at him in the dark, barely able to discern his features. "I trust the Lord to take care of us, too."

"You're not sorry we're here, are you?"

"No. Somehow I feel we were meant to be here, and if that's so, then God will take care of the rest of it."

They fell asleep in each other's arms, with Mary Anna silently talking to God.

The next morning Daniel began his preparation for leaving her. The horses were secured in a paddock, the cows were in their pen, and the outbuildings were secured close by. He looked at Mary Anna confidently. "I'm planning to drive into Stephenville. I'll be gone two days at most. It's a small place, but they should have the things we need." As though to make the trip more important, he added, "Someday it will be a big city."

He held her close for a moment, kissed her gently, patted Columbus on the head, and climbed up into the wagon. His mustache was dark and full, and his teeth looked very white underneath it. "I'll bring you some peppermint, if they have it," he promised.

He looked back over his shoulder to watch the tiny woman in the big poke bonnet holding his son's hand and waving. How he wished he could trust God to watch over his little family! But all he could do was hurry back as quickly as possible to protect them himself.

ʖ

Mary Anna was worried about what might happen to Daniel on the trail, and she prayed with all her heart for their safety. She kept herself twice as busy as usual to make the time go faster. She chose one of her day dresses and began to let it out. It wouldn't be too many months before she'd be needing something larger to wear. She smiled secretly. She hadn't told Daniel yet.

She swept the ground around the outside of the cabin, trying to keep the grass and small trees from coming up. A swept yard was less likely to harbor snakes and other dangerous pests. Then she fussed around her rose bushes. There were four of them, given to her by Louisa.

In the springs of her life, Mary Anna always had special feelings that came over her. It was as if God had made promises all winter long, and now He was about to keep every one of them.

The spring scent she remembered most from her childhood was the perfume of roses. Her stepmother had kept a flower garden and filled the sides along it with herbs for medicine and healing teas. Mary Anna would plant hers, too, someday soon. But for now, she babied the tender rose bushes, watching for the first buds to open and give off their heady aroma.

Columbus was playing close by in the dirt, digging with a spoon, as she dug around the plants. Something in the distance caught her eye, and with a gasp she recognized a ragged band of Indians crossing the rise not far from the woods. Her gun was handy, but there was no need to get it yet. The band had women and children in it, so it wasn't a raiding party. She glanced down at Columbus, talking to him as she would an adult. "Look, there goes a band of Indians." She shook her head sadly. "I don't know how Daniel can hate them now. They look beaten. Everything they own is gone. Pushed from their lands. Locked up on government reservations."

She thought of the story of Cynthia Ann Parker being kidnapped by the Comanches and raised as one of their own. In some ways it was a romantic tale, for it was rumored Cynthia Ann had married a handsome chief and had borne his children. It was also said she was happy with the Comanche, and had hidden for years from those who would come and rescue her. But Mary Anna had heard the other side of the tale, of those who were not adopted by the Comanche but were kept as their slaves. Shivers ran up her spine as some of the awful stories crept into her mind.

The Comanche had been masters of this land only a few years before. Now that the white man had come and killed all the buffalo and broken every promise made to the Indians, the Comanche and the other tribes had been beaten into a subservient feudal system. The government would take care of them from now on. Or so it said.

Mary Anna shook her head and began digging in the dirt. Her feelings were so mixed up. She felt deep sorrow for them when she saw them in rags and destitute, but she was overwhelmed with terrible fear when they were near. She wasn't afraid of the people in this band, but she watched them disappear, just to be sure.

By dusk she was tired and ready to call it a day, but nervous energy kept her moving. She checked the stock and finally pushed the heavy door of the cabin shut and barred it with a thick piece of timber.

Columbus was not a good companion that evening. He fussed and complained with his teething and was generally bad-tempered.

"Taking after your mama, huh?" she accused him gently. After being rocked for a long time, he surrendered to sleep, and Mary Anna read her Bible to take the edge off her uneasiness. She started to take off her clothes and put on her long white nightgown.

"No," she said to her mirror, "if I'm to die tonight, I don't want to be in my nightgown. I want to be ready to defend us." She pulled the baby's bed closer to hers, laid the long rifle on the other side of the bed, and propped herself up on the fat, goose down pillows. "I may not be able to stay awake all night, but I'm as ready as I can be."

The baby slept fitfully, and she dozed between his night noises. Her ears were keenly tuned to any outside sounds. She didn't hear a thing, and was surprised when she woke close to dawn. She and the baby were fine, but she worried about the stock.

Cautiously she lifted the heavy timber and, gun in hand, peeked out toward the outbuildings. Everything looked fine. She could see her cow, the horses, and cattle out in their pens. She took a deep breath of relief and stepped outside the cabin. The sun was just breaking the dark horizon. *Thank You for our safekeeping through the night, Lord.*

Her courage was growing with one successful night behind her. She only had to make it through one more day and night. Daniel would be home for sure after that. She would feed the animals later when she could take Columbus with her. She took one last deep breath of the invigorating air and turned to step back into the cabin.

Her body froze. A moccasin print sat right at her front door! Hurriedly she scanned the area, but nothing was out of place. With her heart pounding like a baby rabbit caught in a coyote's mouth, she carefully checked for more prints. They went all around the cabin.

six

The sixth legislature of Texas had created the county of Erath
in 1856. Stephenville was to be the county seat, named for the
man who had proposed it. The town was laid out with the
public square in the center and the streets named. It was a
town of promise, a wilderness marked from the beginning to
be successful for those accepting the promise, as well as the
challenges, it offered.

Scattered around it were several small communities, all struggling to become a land of plenty for the hearty.

The county abounded with post oak, Spanish oak, wild plum,
pecan, hackberry, and elm trees. Cedar and mesquite were there,
both a bane and a blessing for a cattleman. The cedar would
make good posts, but the mesquite was almost impossible to
clear for crop lands.

Daniel was watchful for Indians, and saw some tracks of
unshod horses that crossed the road. His thoughts went immediately to Mary Anna and the baby. But he had no choice but to
go on as planned.

⁊ø

Mary Anna was mad. Raging mad. She stomped around the
cabin and threw one of her best tea towels at the wall, but her
hand stopped short of the pretty tea cup lying innocently there
on the table. Columbus was watching her with deep interest.

"All they're trying to do is scare me," she fumed. "It's probably those same three raggedy men who were here before. If
they think they can scare me into giving them more meat,
they've got another thought coming!" She kicked at the hap-
less chair in her way and scarred its leg with her shoe.

"Come on, Columbus, we're going out to work in the garden. I'll be double-dipped if they're going to keep me from my vegetables." She grabbed up the baby, the gun, and more ammunition, slammed her poke bonnet on her head, and strode out to her nicely growing garden. Even in her anger she was careful to put on her gloves and pull down the sleeves of her dress to completely cover her from the sun.

Her head was down, but her eyes were like the eyes of a hungry, hunting eagle. Constantly she scanned the horizon and the small buildings around her. Her anger made the weeds fly from her garden, as though she were hacking the Indians out of her life. Her sharp eyes didn't miss Columbus toddling around the edge of the garden, picking up twigs and rocks, and pounding the ground with his wooden spoon. His happy baby talk brought the first smile of the day to her lips. *He's walking so well. Look at him go! He sees something. Look at him go!* She traced his path with her eyes to see what had so attracted him. Her heart stopped.

At the edge of the garden about ten feet from her baby sat a coiled rattler. Columbus was heading straight for it. It never occurred to Mary Anna that she might miss hitting the deadly snake with the gun. She simply cocked it and took very careful aim. Even the beads of sweat that should have clouded her aim were of no consequence. If she didn't hit the snake, it would hit Columbus. She fired, knowing she wouldn't have time to reload. The mangled head of the snake flew off, and Columbus began to cry. Mary Anna sprinted over to him and swept him up with grateful arms.

"Thank You, Lord. Oh, dear God, thank You!" Her heart pounded and her legs turned rubbery. She slumped to the ground with Columbus on her lap and gulped down deep breaths. Was there no end to the dangers that surrounded her? Why had it been so much easier when Daniel was with her? If only he'd come home! She refused to consider what might happen if he didn't. Only God could keep them alive in this suddenly un-friendly place.

She took her crying child into the cabin and sat with him in her lap, rocking him for a long, long time. Finally they both settled down.

She could hear the pitiful lowing of the cow that hadn't been milked. Much as Mary Anna was tempted to spend the rest of the day in the relative security of her cabin, she had work to do.

Columbus had fallen asleep, and she took her shawl and made a sling across her chest to carry him in. She got the rifle, reloaded it, and put on her bonnet again. She walked out to the cow pen with her back straight and her eyes darting around.

"I'm sorry to be so late, Daisy, but things have been a little busy today," she said as she patted the cow and settled herself down on the milking stool. "I'm asking you very nicely, please don't knock the milk pail over or step in it. I'm not sure what I'd do if one more thing happened today."

Daisy was compliant, but the chickens acted spooked and extra squawky as Mary Anna scattered seed for them. She didn't act hurried, in case someone was watching her, but she worked efficiently so she could get back to the safety of the cabin.

After the quick noon meal, she locked the cabin door and tried to nap with Columbus. She dozed fitfully, waking with a start and then trying to sleep again. It was not restful.

The remainder of the afternoon, Mary Anna stayed inside the cabin, pulling the rocker where she could look out the door and see the woods. She carded wool and spun it into thread for clothes. Columbus woke happy and hungry and played with abandonment on the floor, unaware of his close call with the rattlesnake.

When dusk came, Mary Anna took Columbus out to the cow pen and milked Daisy again, staying as calm as possible so she wouldn't alarm the cow. It would take twice as long to milk a nervous cow, and she didn't have that kind of time.

With a sigh of relief, she finished the chores and dropped the timber across the door of the cabin. Now all she had to do was get through the night.

Much to her chagrin, she woke the next morning without having awakened once during the night. Columbus was still sleeping as she went through the ritual of opening the cabin and checking for tracks. New footprints stood at her door.

She looked toward the cow pen and saw Daisy chewing contentedly. But when she tried to count the horses, it seemed one was missing. She couldn't be sure about the cattle, and she couldn't check unless she went out there. Gingerly she hurried out. Yes, one horse was missing. Her Irish temper fired up full blast.One of the most important things she had been taught as a child was that if it wasn't yours, you didn't even touch it, much less take it.

It isn't fair! she shouted internally. But she walked sedately to the cabin. She had done everything in her power to keep the animals safe, but she couldn't sleep with them. "Oh, why didn't we bring a dog with us?" she wailed inside the walls of her safety. "He could have warned me." She laughed sheepishly at herself. "And then what would you have done, gone running out there and blasted the thieves?" She poured a cup of black coffee and added a splash of cream. "At least it would have scared them off," she consoled herself. "Maybe."

Once again the day had gotten off to a bad start. "I'm never going to let Daniel leave again. Next time I'll go and he can stay home," she said flatly.

She was about to leave the cabin to go to the spring for water when two Indian men rode up. They were not the ragged men she had seen before. As they approached, Mary Anna barely had time to whisper, "Dear Lord, in heaven, help me!"

These men were astride beautiful pinto ponies. Her first impression of them was one of complete elegance. They were dressed in fringed buckskin and seemed to be extensions of their horses. Had Mary Anna known about the riding abilities of the Comanches, she could have identified the men at once.

Their braids were astonishingly long and well cared for, each tied off with strips of fur. A single black feather was rakishly stuck in one man's side lock, and both were wearing necklaces of animal claws. The tops of their ears had been pierced in many places, and long, thin shells dangled down, pulling the ears over slightly with their weight.

The center parts of their hair were daubed in red, and their faces had circles and lines of yellow and white. They presented a breathtaking sight—and a fearsome one.

Mary Anna stood rooted in place, quietly watching the men come closer. There was something odd about their faces. And as they sat arrogantly ten feet away, she realized they had no eyebrows. They had either been plucked or shaved off completely. It gave them a more menacing look.

Her hand was resting lightly on the rifle leaning against the side of the cabin. Columbus was inside.

The silent stand-off was broken when one of the men spoke. "I am called Swift-as-the-Antelope." He waited for a counter introduction.

"I am Mary Anna Garland Thornton." His name was so long, she felt the need to include everything she could in her introduction.

Each was sizing up the other, and Mary Anna showed absolutely no fear.

"I am here to trade with you."

"What did you bring to trade?" Mary Anna could see no goods.

"I will trade you the safety of your horses for sugar and meat."

The audacity of the man almost made Mary Anna gasp audibly.

"I have meat to trade, but no sugar." She took a deep breath and added in a clipped tone, "You already owe me for one horse." She didn't know for a fact that these men had taken the horse, but she was so angry, she didn't care.

She waited for him to pull out a tomahawk or bow and arrow and kill her on the spot for the rude charges she had made against them.

Swift-as-the-Antelope considered for a moment and then spoke. "Then I will take only the meat." He made it sound as if he were doing her a favor.

Mary Anna considered her options and decided under the circumstances, she had little choice. "Wait here," she ordered.

She walked casually into the cabin on quivering legs and retrieved a large package containing the smoked antelope haunch they had put up. She took it outside. The Comanche warrior leaned slightly from his horse and took the meat. Without a visible sign from their riders, both horses broke into a trot, heading for the forest.

Mary Anna walked into the cabin and locked the door again. She was exhilarated from a successful encounter with the Indians, weak with relief that she was still alive, and breathless with fear. "I can't live like this, Lord. Give me courage and wisdom. And please keep these people away from my door, no matter how magnificent they look."

She went out only to milk the cow. She didn't count the horses or check on the cattle. It wouldn't do any good. The rest of the time she kept the door locked and worked inside. Then she began to worry about Daniel. He should already be back.

"Be calm," she told herself. "You know how things are out here. He didn't promise to be back today. He said he'd *try* to be back today. You can make it one more night. He'll surely be back in the morning."

The pounding on the door would have made her heart completely stop if it hadn't been accompanied by the shouting of her name.

"Mary Anna, open up, I'm home!"

And then they were in each other's arms, hugging and laughing. Columbus toddled over and grabbed hold of his father's leg, hugging it hard, until an adolescent dog of indeterminable heritage came running in. He immediately began to lick and play with Columbus. The boy was enchanted.

Mary Anna was so happy and relieved to see Daniel that at first she didn't notice the man standing in the doorway, holding his hat in his hand.

She looked at Daniel expectantly.

"Oh, I'm so sorry. Mary Anna this is Otto Lammert. He's going to be working for us."

Otto stepped forward and made a slight bow. "Nice to meet ya, Miz Thornton." He spoke in a heavy Texas twang.

"And I am delighted to meet you, Mr. Lammert." She thought him to be in his late twenties. He was lanky and wiry, long and relaxed, and strong. She liked him immediately. He was shy in front of her and kept twirling his beaten-up hat in his hands.

"Well, come on in, Mr. Lammert." She looked at Daniel. "Have you eaten?"

"Thank you, yes. Otto shot us a fine bird." He smiled at his wife. "He is an excellent shot."

Otto grinned like a kid and kicked his toe in the dirt floor.

But Mary Anna's face began to burn with anger. "Good, we're going to need him. The Indians stole one of the horses, and two more men have been by here for meat."

Daniel looked at her in deadly calm and walked over to the table to sit down. Otto followed him. "Tell me from the beginning."

While Columbus romped with the playful puppy, Mary Anna told her story. "The only satisfaction I got out of giving the meat away was that it was an antelope haunch, and I hope every time Swift-as-the-Antelope takes a bite, he feels a pain in his behind!"

Daniel didn't smile, but she saw an amused glimmer in Otto's eyes.

"Miz Thornton, you were safe at night. Them Comanches are superstitious, and they won't come in on you in the night. But them horses and cows is another thing. They're used to hunting and they feel free to cut out whatever they want. You wuz prob'ly smart giving them the meat."

"There won't be any more of that, Otto. I'm not going to be blackmailed anymore. I'm not a government agent, and I'm not a store. Let 'em stay on the reservation. They've no right to my possessions." Daniel's face had the dark look Mary Anna had seen when he'd talked about his grandfather. "And there won't be any more missing horses," he promised. He grabbed up his hat. "Come on, Otto, let's check the stock and make sure the horses are up close to the cow pen."

"I'll bunk down there in the shed tonight."

While the men did what they could to insure the safety of the stock, Mary Anna knelt down to the puppy. "I haven't given you a proper welcome yet, but I am so glad to see you. What shall we name him, Columbus?"

At the sound of her voice, the dog put his front paws up on her lap and gave her a wet welcome with his soft tongue. He was mostly black with white patches here and there. "You're going to be our guard. I think I'll call you Soldier." She hugged him close. "You have your work cut out for you, Soldier."

She heard the men coming back from their inspection. She had been so excited to see Daniel, and then to tell him what had happened, she had forgotten the treasures he was bringing. As they brought in the goods, she stored them.

While Otto was out getting the last of it, Daniel pulled out a brown paper-wrapped package. "This is for you. I know you're going to be needing material to make baby clothes, so I bought the best flannel they had." His face was split with a big grin by the surprise he saw on hers. "Surely you didn't think I wouldn't know?" he teased softly.

Daniel stood there with that silly grin on his face watching her open the package like a kid on Christmas Day. It slipped badly when he saw the disappointed look on her face. "It's the best flannel they had," he said lamely.

She looked at him helplessly. She had a boy already and she was thinking of the sweet little girl things she would make this time, for surely the child would be a girl. "It's the best flannel I ever saw, but Daniel, *red* flannel?"

"It was the only color they had," he shrugged.

She recovered from the shock, appreciated his thoughtfulness, and then began to laugh and hug him. "Thank you, my darling, for bringing me the fabric. We'll have the most cheerful baby in the whole state of Texas!"

He was reassured by her quick recovery. "I might have bought enough for you to make me a new pair of long johns, too," he grinned.

seven

Mary Anna woke at her usual time and smiled broadly to find Daniel watching her from his pillow. "You're sure nicer to sleep with than that big old rifle," she said.

"You have the whitest skin and the softest hair I've ever seen." He brushed her cheek with his fingertip.

"And you look so handsome with your dark mustache. It's getting so thick, but it's soft. My grandfather's was stiff and bristly."

"It's because it's never been shaved." Daniel was just taking her in his arms when Columbus awkwardly climbed into bed with them, and Soldier, hearing the happy noises, jumped in the middle of all of them.

"Get off this bed, you mangy mutt," growled Daniel as he swept Soldier off with his arm. "Today you start learning how to behave." His tone was gruff, but Mary Anna wasn't fooled. He was pleased as punch to have Soldier around, and he'd train the dog to protect them and their animals.

Mary Anna got out of bed and began to dress. The days were getting warmer, and she decided on a whim to leave off one of her petticoats.

She brushed her hair out and twisted it up quickly, securing it with hair pins. Daniel's compliment had made her happy. Even in this wilderness, she went through her usual toilette and was extremely careful never to let the sun touch her skin. She used lard on her hands to keep them soft, in spite of the rough work she did.

Lord, she prayed, *I know I'm vain, but I thank You for making me attractive. Help me not to care so much about how I look. And help me with my temper*. It was a prayer she prayed frequently. So far the Lord hadn't made her less vain, but she wasn't sure how He'd go about that. She patted her hair smoothly and hurried to her daily chores.

Daniel brought Otto with him for breakfast. Mary Anna served her cottage-cheese flour bread along with a hearty helping of fried meat and all the eggs she had gathered from her small flock of laying hens.

"Nothing like the smell of fresh ground coffee cooking in the morning," Daniel said happily. Mary Anna stood by his side as she said their mealtime prayer. Columbus was sitting in a high chair pushed up to one side of the table, banging his spoon.

"You have a fine looking son there, Miz Thornton," said Otto politely.

"You get an extra helping of eggs for that kind observation," she chuckled.

He buttered the bread and took a large bite. As he chewed, he got a quizzical look on his face. "This here is a most unusual tasting bread."

Daniel and Mary Anna broke into laughter, and Daniel explained why he had gone on the trip to Stephenville.

"How did you wind up in Stephenville?" asked Mary Anna.

"Well, now, ma'am, Stephenville wasn't my original destination. I wuz headed for Louzeanna."

Mary Anna laughed, "But that's the other way."

"Yessum, I'm plum bad about directions." He enjoyed entertaining people with his implausible stories. "My family came from Germany and settled down close to the coast of Texas. Their ship got knocked off course, and they landed in the wrong place. Seems we've been doing it ever since."

He took a big bite of his food, chewed thoughtfully, wiped his mouth and added, "I heared this part of Texas was the place to ranch now that the Injuns were pretty well taken ker of." He looked solemnly at Mary Anna. "I'm here to tell you it ain't so. You be kerful, little lady. You ain't been out here long enough to know the good Injuns from the bad uns."

Mary Anna was afraid Daniel was going to mouth the old saying about all Indians being bad Indians, but he caught the look in her eye and took another big bite of his food.

"I think it would be a good move to keep trading with them Injuns if all they want is food. You might call it a peace policy, but while I was in Stephenville, I found out half the federal troops left here to guard this part of the frontier is gone, and the Comanches have been pretty well raiding anywhere they please. When those thirty-three hunert men was here to watch them, they didn't dare bother the settlers. Now there's not enough men to keep them under control, and they're like hungry wolves. Long as they're only trading, you'd best do it. We're a mite short-handed out here on your place."

Otto could tell this didn't sit well with his new boss, but he knew the truth and had stayed alive because he was a smart man. Daniel reluctantly shook his head in agreement.

"But trade is what we'll do. No more stealing from us."

"There's jest one other little thing I thought I might mention to ya. The Comanches and Apaches go up north on the Llano Estacado for the winter. No one knows exactly where. They jest seem to disappear clean out of sight. Before the white men killed so many of the buffalo, they followed them. And when they felt like doing a little raidin' they rode on down into Mexico. If I took a map and drew a line from the Llano to Mexico, you'd be sitting in the middle of their road."

Mary Anna felt the hair rise on her arms and the back of her neck. Daniel looked grim.

"It's true a lot of 'em are on reservations in the territory north of us, and some on the Brazos. But they ain't no where near ready to give up yet. So that's why I say we should try to git along with 'em as best we can. And always be ready to defend ourselves."

"Well, then," said Daniel, "we'd better get to work. We'll be needing more meat, and I want to strengthen our fences." He looked at Otto.

Mary Anna said, "Guess the Lord was the one who got you lost so we could find you."

"Yes, ma'am." He smiled at Mary Anna. "But I've never been knowed to git myself lost on the way to such a good table, ma'am."

Mary Anna hummed happily while the men worked outside. She felt safe and happy. But she continued to be alert, for she took to heart the things Otto had told them.

A week or so passed before they came in contact with the Indians again. It was getting close to dusk and the men were cleaning up at the basin outside the cabin when a young Indian man dressed only in breechclouts came riding in on a thin pony. A young girl sat behind him. They waited for Daniel to approach them.

Mary Anna was embarrassed by his nakedness, yet fascinated with his bronzed skin. She saw that the young girl was in the last months of her pregnancy. She was also shocked when she estimated the girl to be about fourteen years old.

She was wearing a buckskin skirt, a loose-fitting blouse, and moccasins. Her cropped hair gave her the appearance of an adolescent boy rather than a young mother-to-be, but there was no mistaking the familiar bulge in the front of her skirt. She didn't have the same sun-burned color skin as her husband, though she was deeply tanned. Mary Anna looked with disbelief into eyes the same color as her own.

Her first thought was that the girl was being held captive, but as she observed the trading going on between the men, Mary Anna detected no sign that the girl was in any way trying to escape the handsome warrior. She sat easily on the pony, waiting patiently.

Mary Anna clenched her teeth in sadness. This could only be a child who had been kidnapped from her family and raised as a Comanche. Somewhere a mother's heart was breaking not knowing the fate of her child. Mary Anna shuddered as she thought about the dark hand that had touched Columbus' hair. The girl was much too young to be Cynthia Ann Parker, but it appeared she was the second chapter of that familiar story of white girls being captured and raised as Comanches.

&

The next three days they were cabin-bound by the spring rains that soaked the earth. There was plenty of time for Mary Anna and Daniel to learn more about the Comanches from Otto.

"They ain't nothing without their horses, but you put a horse underneath one of 'em and they become a thing of beauty." His eyes clouded with memories. "I was in a freight wagon down around Austin once when they hit us. They're fierce fighters and they use their horses as shields. Come in hangin' off the side and shoot from underneath its neck. Don't give ya much of a target. And I've seen 'em swoop down and pick up their dead or wounded. They never leave any behind." Mary Anna saw goose flesh rise along his arm where his sleeve was rolled up. "The screaming and yelling they do as they come in at ya is enough to scare the hair right off yer head, 'less they lift it first."

"Do they really scalp people?" She couldn't imagine a more grisly activity.

He nodded solemnly. "But it gives 'um more honor to do it when they're in battle. I knew a man that survived it. Had a fearsome bald spot from the front of his head to the back. Ugly scar. They try to git as close to the enemy as possible. If they touch him or kill him, they get to count coup. That's real important to how the other warriors look at him."

"What about captives?" Daniel asked.

"Never keep the men, only women and young'uns. Usually

trade the women off and raise the kids. Make Comanches out of 'em. Use the girls quick as they can as breeding stock, beggin' your pardon, ma'am."

Mary Anna felt her own flesh rise in horror.

Ominous thunder rolled across the land and shook the logs of their cabin with its vibrations.

"Them Injuns is all huddled in their tepees today. That's the one thing they're scairt of, thunder and lightning." He took out a pocket knife and began whittling on a piece of fire wood. "The government is going to have to do something about 'em before too long. Too many white folks want to get on with their settlin'. They need the protection of the troops."

"You know a lot about the Indians," Mary Anna observed.

"It's the best way to stay alive." He looked steadily at her. "In some ways I admire 'em a bunch. But I just don't understand their minds about killing and torturing." He sighed. "The whole thing is a big mess. Seems like growed men could get together and divide up the land in a way to make everybody happy."

Mary Anna asked quietly, "Would you want someone to come to your ranch and divide it up equally for you?"

"I know what yer saying, ma'am. But this land isn't a ranch. It's a big piece of free land, rich for living on and using." Daniel nodded his head in agreement. "Miz Thornton, I hope the day doesn't come when something awful will happen to you or yer loved ones that will make you think like I do. I admire the way you feel about the Injuns, but you're a tenderfoot out here." He looked sympathetically at her. "I hope life doesn't change your mind." He didn't sound optimistic about that.

❧

April was a sweet month, spent in tending crops, gathering the first tender vegetables, and feeling the fluttering of the child within her. The whole land was bursting with fruitfulness, and

Mary Anna felt a part of it.

There had been no sign of Indians for weeks.

"I want to go out into the forest and gather berries," she said off-handedly to Daniel at breakfast.

"I can't go with you today, and neither can Otto."

"If you can keep an eye on Columbus, I can manage the pails and the gun."

He looked at her as if she were crazy. "You know that's where we always see them."

"I don't plan to go in far, and I don't want to live like a scared ninny." Her chin jutted out in that defiant way he knew so well.

"I can work on the fields closest to the woods," he said, "but you better watch what's going on all around you. Be real quiet and listen." His face held a dire warning of what would happen if she didn't follow his orders. She took him seriously, but she was excited to get away from the cabin for a while.

She struck out across the roughly planed log that served as a bridge across the stream and headed into the forest. Instead of the rifle, she was carrying the Colt revolver in her apron pocket.

It was cool in the woods. She was cautious as she headed for the places close by that promised berries. At first she could hear the beating of her own heart at being alone, but the gun gave her confidence.

She walked quickly to a small hollow deep in the trees where red haws were likely to grow. She froze when a movement caught her eye. There in the hollow sat the pregnant young girl with whom they had traded earlier. Mary Anna looked around for her husband, but the girl was alone.

She slipped her hand into her apron pocket and curled her fingers around the revolver as she watched the young girl. Her eyes were glazed with pain. She was in labor and alone. Mary Anna wanted to help her, but something in the girl's manner stopped her.

The girl put a rolled piece of rawhide between her teeth and rocked on her heels silently as a contraction racked her young body. She panted, and her brow broke out in perspiration. Her buckskin skirt was hiked up, and she was squatting over a piece of tanned hide filled with a soft rabbit skin. Stoically she pushed with the next contraction. No sound came from her as she strained with the contractions that rhythmically rocked her body. She grabbed hold of the tree in front of her and gave one last gigantic push which delivered the head of her child.

The black hair was plastered wetly against its tiny head, and the girl lay down to finish her delivery. With the next contraction she gently pulled the child out and lay the little boy in her lap. He let out a loud squall as she wiped his face clean with a soft rag. Using a piece of rawhide, she tied the umbilical cord and cut it, and delivered the placenta with one final push.

Awestricken, Mary Anna watched the girl clean the baby carefully with oil and wrap him tightly in soft wrappings. Tucking him up under her blouse and securing the bottom in her skirt, she rose and walked to a small pool of water to clean herself. Then she dug a deep hole and dropped in the afterbirth with the birthing mat and covered it. The girl peeked inside her blouse and the smallest of smiles flitted across her face. Proudly she picked up her small package of things and walked serenely into the deeper woods.

Mary Anna felt weak and exultant at the same time. She leaned against the tree and tried to sort out the dramatic tableau that had unfolded in front of her.

A young child-mother had silently delivered herself in the woods. If Mary Anna had ever worried about what would happen when her own time came, she dismissed such thoughts now. This was her second child, and if there was no one there to deliver her, she, too, would deliver herself.

It was a wiser and older Mary Anna who walked back to the cabin later in the afternoon, her bucket overflowing with rich, red berries and her heart overflowing with respect for a silent young Comanche girl and her new baby.

She didn't share her experience with Daniel. It was too precious to put into words. She wasn't even sure he would understand what had happened, and he wouldn't be happy to know there were still Indians nearby. Instinctively she knew they were of no threat to their safety. In fact, they were probably miles away by now.

She found herself more tender with Columbus and Daniel. Life was dear, and the life she carried inside her was a real treasure. She longed to be able to hold the child close to her as she had seen the young girl do.

❧

While Mary Anna concentrated on her garden and Columbus, Daniel decided to add to their poultry supply by capturing some of the numerous wild turkeys in the area. "We'll have so many more eggs," he promised her.

"But how are you going to catch them?"

His smile was sly. "I have a plan. First Otto and I are going to build a coop for them."

Mary Anna had watched the turkeys perch on the low branches of trees, but they were easily alarmed and could fly for short distances. She gave her husband an encouraging smile, "I hope the plan will work."

Otto was silent as they made the coop. He thought it was a foolish thing to try, but Daniel was his boss, so he kept his mouth shut. He didn't like the taste of the turkey meat, and was fairly certain he wouldn't like their eggs either.

When the day arrived to capture the birds, Mary Anna took Columbus along and planned to gather any eggs they might find while the men did the hard work.

The plan called for each man to be on opposite sides of a known roosting place. When Otto came in from one way and Daniel the other, they would grab whatever bird came their way and stuff it in a sack. Mary Anna and Columbus hid down low, waiting.

She could see Otto sneaking up from his side and Daniel gliding though the brush from the other side. There were some birds on the ground pecking for food and some roosting on the low branches of several trees. Closer and closer the men came to the unsuspecting turkeys.

All at once the birds began squawking and screaming and flapping their powerful wings. Some flew, and some ran, and all attacked anything that came near them.

Daniel was desperately holding on to the legs of one big male while the turkey beat him with his wings and pecked viciously at his hands. Columbus began to cry at all the cacophony of screaming. Birds flew and ran in all directions. Otto was hot on the trail of a big fat hen. He grabbed for her neck and she turned and attacked his face with her sharp beak. He was trying to hold on with one hand, stuff her in the sack with the other, and duck his head to protect his face.

At first Mary Anna was frightened for the men and unnerved by the wild fear of the turkeys. Then she began to laugh and couldn't stop herself even when Daniel shot her an angry look.

"Help me," he shouted.

She couldn't have helped if she'd wanted to, for she was holding her sides and laughing helplessly at the flying dirt and feathers.

When the dust settled, Daniel had one turkey in his sack and Otto had two. They fell to the ground in exhaustion and looked foolishly at one another. "I think there's got to be a better way to do this," Daniel said with chagrin.

Otto wiped the blood from his face with a dirty hand. "Let's forget catching them and just shoot them from now on."

Mary Anna came rushing over to the two men. "I had no idea turkeys were so strong and mean. Are you all right?"

"I'd be better if you hadn't laughed at me," grumped Daniel.

"But you should have seen it from my side," she grinned. "You two rest here while I check for nests." There was a cutting edge to her next remarks. "I'll try to keep these eggs warm and hatch them. Domesticated fowl are so much more tender. And safer."

There was no discussion about whether to try the plan again. The little band went home with their small bounty and turned the mad birds into the coop.

Daniel and Otto built a barn for the horses and raised the fences higher around the pasture. They added a room to the cabin for Otto and dug a root cellar close to the house.

Otto chose to sleep in the little lean-to out by the barn when the weather was warmer. Soldier stayed out there, and with them on guard there was no more trouble from marauding Indians.

While the men gathered the crops, Mary Anna put up everything she could for the winter. There was a good harvest, and the family contemplated the long winter stretching out in front of them with satisfaction. Daniel cured meat and carefully wrapped it for storage. He saved seed for next year's crops.

Summer turned to the last hot days of August and then to the crisp mornings of September. The trees started to have a faint yellow tinge as they began their rest from the summer heat. Splashes of orange could be seen in the tops of the trees across the stream, and an occasional deep purple from the maple trees stood out in marked contrast. The seasons were slowing down, and so was Mary Anna.

She spent more time sewing. They had planted cotton, but the bolls wouldn't pop open until there was a good cold snap. Then she would card the seeds from the bolls, twist the fluff into thread, and weave it into cloth on her loom.

She fashioned a shapeless tunic for herself. The loose-fitting, floor-length shift was comfortable and needed no alterations as she grew. Her feet tended to swell toward the end of the day, and she longed for a pair of larger shoes. Rather than bother Daniel with her needs, she cut up some of the tanned hides they had gotten in trade with the last Indian visitors and made soft moccasins for herself. As she worked on the leather, she wondered how the young mother and child were and if they would survive the coming winter.

The moccasins were not the works of art turned out by the true craftsmen of the Plains, but they felt wonderful on her feet.

Daniel was not as pleased as she was. "Where did you get those shoes?" he demanded.

"I made them. My feet are swelling, and I can't bear to wear my shoes anymore."

"They make you look like an Indian squaw. I'll get you another pair of real shoes." His face reflected the displeasure in his voice.

"But there's no need," she protested. "These feel wonderful. They're so soft, and they didn't cost anything but the time I spent making them." She had her chin stuck out slightly in the way that meant she was not ready to back down docilely to what she considered an unreasonable request.

Daniel noted the tilt of her chin and gave the offending shoes a hateful stare. Silently he stalked to the door and slammed it hard behind him.

Mary Anna felt the roots of her hair begin to burn with anger. She walked to the cabin door and opened it wide, giving it a loud slam of her own. She moved heatedly around the small cabin, pacing her anger. "That man! Why should I be uncomfortable because he doesn't like Indians? I can't wear moccasins because his grandfather was killed by an Indian years ago? This makes perfect sense to me," she added sarcastically.

"Here's your dinner," she told her absent husband as she slammed it on the table. "I hope it gives you as much indigestion as it does me."

In the last stages of her pregnancy, everything gave her indigestion, and her anger made things worse, so she drank a little milk, made up a little lunch for Columbus, and said, "Come on, baby, we're going on a picnic." She was especially careful to slam the cabin door again as she left.

Columbus was pleased to be walking alongside his panting mother on an aimless stroll. They walked down by the turkey pen with Soldier trotting along. She had the revolver in her apron pocket. Even the remembered story of the ill-fated turkey hunt failed to make her smile.

She took Columbus down by the stream where she let him play at the edge of the water, helping him toss rocks in its shiny face. She stayed away as long as she could, hoping that by the time she got back Daniel would already have eaten and gone back to his work. She didn't want to see him or be near him.

When she finally opened the door to the cabin, she half expected to see the back of her angry husband. The cabin was empty and the food was on the table untouched. *He's really mad.*

She sat down in the rocker while Columbus played. Her unborn child kicked and played, too. She could just see the tips of her feet when she sat in the chair.

What happened? I was uncomfortable and I made some shoes. Daniel got mad because they make me look like an Indian. A pair of shoes has come between us. She sighed. *They aren't worth it. I'll go barefooted. It won't be long until the baby comes. How stupid to fight over something this trivial!* She rose tiredly and made up a picnic basket of the lunch things. She silently laughed when she thought of Otto. *He missed his dinner, and he doesn't even know why.*

She started for the fields and met Daniel coming up to the house.

"I thought you and Otto might be hungry," she began a little nervously. He met her eyes and she said, "I'm sorry, Daniel."

Her words overlapped his words of apology, and they threw themselves into each other's arms.

"I won't wear the shoes. You're right, I do need new ones. Winter will be here soon."

"I was silly to be so angry over them. Wear them. I know your feet hurt. I'll get you some winter ones."

"We let a pair of shoes come between us," she said softly.

"I know. After I got over my anger, that's all I could think of. A pair of shoes." Their laughter was low and intimate.

"Dinner, Otto," Daniel shouted and waved at the hard-working man. "Thank you for the lunch," he said tenderly. "I'm sure Otto is as hungry as I am, and he didn't even know why he wasn't getting fed."

With a soft kiss, Mary Anna left and smiled her way back to the cabin. Columbus had crawled up into her bed and fallen asleep. Peacefully Mary Anna lay back in the rocker for a cat nap, and then she planned to fix Daniel and Otto a special meal. The moccasins had been hidden away in the big trunk. *Thank You, Lord, for giving me such a good husband,* she prayed as she closed her eyes.

Two long, hot days passed, and Mary Anna thought of the family she had left behind. She even missed Louisa. She hadn't heard the voice of another woman in eight months, and the only people she had been with were Daniel and Otto. This was the time of year her family usually had a big get-together to celebrate the gathering of the crops. There would be dancing and laughter and too much to eat and drink. In her mind's eye she could see her sisters talking excitedly as they used rag strips to put up their hair in curls to dry and chose their prettiest dresses. The whole town would be together.

She served supper with many sighs and no smiles. She picked at her food, and was short with Columbus. Daniel and Otto exchanged furtive looks.

Otto cleared his throat. "This is a very good supper, Miz Thornton."

She nodded absent-mindedly.

Daniel tried. "You should have seen Soldier chasing rabbits this afternoon. He found a whole nest of them and when they scattered, he couldn't make up his mind which one to chase." He chuckled and Otto chuckled. She sighed.

After supper the two men huddled under the tree in the front yard.

"Is it almost time?" Otto asked.

"Not for more than another month."

He shook his head and chewed on his lip. "She's homesick, sure as shooting."

"I can't do anything about that." This time Daniel sighed.

"The summer work's mostly done. Can you take her into Stephenville?"

"Why would I want to do that? There's nothing there but a store and a few people. I sure don't want to take her to a store when I don't have any money to buy her anything."

"Will he trade?"

"Maybe, but I don't want to drive a day to find out."

Daniel took a deep breath and sighed through pursed lips.

Otto interrupted his reverie. "I think she's got cabin fever." He looked a little fearfully at Daniel. "One time I worked for a family where the woman got real bad cabin fever."

"What did they do about it?"

"Didn't. She jest dried up and died."

Daniel thought very hard. "If she's homesick, we should find her someone to talk to besides us. A little visit of sorts. You know of any other settlers around here?"

"I heared there wuz a family about five miles north of here. Maybe six."

"Wife, too?"

Otto nodded. "Wife, too."

Their eyes met in silent assent. "I'll watch the place while you take her." He grinned a little. "I don't get cabin fever. I think it's jest a woman thing."

Mary Anna grabbed Daniel around the neck and almost squeezed his breath away. "Visiting! Oh, my, what will I wear?" She hurried over to the trunk and began digging around. "I can't wear this old thing. Where's that dress I wore with Columbus? I'm sure I packed it. It's so pretty. It has lace around the collar. I think I can still get into it."

Daniel stood watching her with a satisfied grin on his face. Cabin fever wasn't hard to cure after all.

Early the next morning, Mary Anna was a blur of busyness. She insisted Daniel go with her to the stream where she could bathe. They hung up blankets in the bushes to afford her more privacy. She usually did this once a week by herself, but she was getting ungainly and she needed help with Columbus. "Well," she demanded, as she undressed down to her bodice and bloomers and stepped into the water. "Bring the baby and get in here."

Daniel started to protest, but he shucked his clothes to his bright new red long johns and tucked the revolver up under his hat as he jammed it on his head. There was always the chance of water moccasins.

Otto could hear the family scrubbing and laughing and playing. It was a good sound. Even if he didn't get cabin fever, he was happier living with the Thorntons than by himself.

When Daniel got up out of the water, he reached for his clothes.

"Oh, no! Don't put on those dirty things! I have clean ones laid out for you on the bed," Mary Anna said.

"But that's a long way from here," Daniel said reasonably.

"I've already thought of that," Mary Anna replied triumphantly.

Otto thought his eyes were playing tricks on him when he

saw Daniel and Mary Anna wrapped in blankets and march-ing quickly to the cabin. The look Daniel gave him kept Otto from making the comment on the tip of his tongue, but it didn't wipe the huge smile off his face.

So a scrubbed and happy family went calling on their neigh-bors. Mary Anna was carrying two pies and smoked meat. She had no idea what shape the other family was in, and she didn't want the Thorntons to put a burden on their new friends.

They approached a cabin that looked pretty much like the one they had left behind. A man stood at the front door, quiet-ing three alarmed dogs. They sat respectfully at their master's feet as Daniel climbed down from the wagon.

Mary Anna's eyes searched for the man's wife.

"Howdy," said the man. He was about Daniel's age, but much thinner. "Y'all climb down and come in out of the heat." He came over to help Mary Anna out of the wagon. He put out a wizened hand to Daniel. "Caleb West." He led the way to the door where Mary Anna could finally see his wife in the dim-ness. She was wiping her hands on her apron and had a shy smile on her broad face. "Howdy," she said quietly.

The woman was about the same age as Mary Anna, but much taller and a bit stout. Behind her skirts hung a boy about four years old, peeking at the visitors. "I'm Virginia West," she said in a deep Southern drawl. "This is Albert." She hurried to a rocker and indicated it for Mary Anna. "Here, sit, sit. Make yourself comfortable."

The men sat at the table and Virginia pulled a chair close to Mary Anna. They had cooled sassafras tea and thick slabs of bread with large plops of apple butter on top. Columbus toddled over to Albert and hugged him hard enough to knock him to the floor, and their friendship was established. Albert took Columbus over to his part of the small cabin to play.

There was no awkwardness in their first minutes together. Virginia was an able hostess, and Caleb was completely at ease.

The men drifted outside to look over the property.

"When's your baby due?" asked Virginia.

"About the end of November." Mary Anna watched the little boys play on the floor together, one so blond and one a bright redhead. "Your little boy is precious."

"Thank you." Without bitterness she added, "We had a girl. Two she was, like your boy. She died of the fever last winter. I just found out I'm going to have another one in about six months."

Mary Anna saw the mixed pain and happiness in Virginia's eyes.

"I'm sorry about your little girl, but happy you're having another one."

"We all know you can never replace a child lost, but I am hoping this one will be a girl for me."

"So am I! Daniel and I both would like this one to be a girl."

Virginia laughed. "I doubt that. Men need sons to help them with their work. The more sons, the more work that gets done without hiring someone."

Mary Anna was offended that Virginia had contradicted her. Daniel had told her he hoped for a girl for her, but she held her tongue. It was true that men needed sons.

"When it comes your time, I'll be glad to come help out," Virginia offered.

"Thank you, and I will do the same for you."

They talked of babies and cooking and recipes, and finally Mary Anna told Virginia the story of the young Comanche girl giving birth in the woods. She watched her new friend's face closely for her reaction.

"There's a lot of folks that hate the Indians for what they've done," Virginia mused. "Personally, I think maybe we're the ones that ought to be saying, 'I'm sorry for messing up your lands.'" She looked directly into Mary Anna's face, trying to read if she had gone too far with this new friend.

Mary Anna grabbed her hands delightedly. "Virginia, I never thought to meet anyone like you in this place. That's how I feel exactly." Softly she asked, "Does your husband feel that way, too?"

Virginia shook her head sadly. "Caleb is the one who wanted to come out here, not me. He seems to think the Indians are wasting the land and he's the one God Himself has chosen to save it from the loss. But he's my husband, so I agreed to come. The price has been high. We lost our daughter, and Caleb hasn't been too well. He had the fever, too. It took a lot out of him. Guess if I'd had it, we'd all be dead. The Lord spared me."

"Why do the men feel this way?" Mary Anna asked.

Virginia shook her head, and Mary Anna guiltily changed the subject. Perhaps she had been disloyal to Daniel in sharing her feelings so openly with a comparative stranger.

When supper time came, Daniel offered the meat and the pies. The Wests were delighted with the additional food, and the dinner talk was lively.

Daniel watched Mary Anna across the table animatedly talking with Virginia and laughing. And he made a promise to himself that she would never get cabin fever again.

The men went outside for one last check of the place. Caleb was the first to speak. "You had any trouble with the Indians yet?"

"A little. Stole one of my horses. Beg me for meat. You?"

"Mostly the same things. I have to tell you, though, I think there's going to be more. Be extra careful."

Daniel nodded his head. He agreed with Caleb, though he hadn't shared his concerns with Mary Anna. "We'll be sleeping out here in the wagon. I'll sleep with one eye open tonight."

"You won't have to. I'll leave you my three dogs. They'll give you plenty of warning."

The night passed without incident, but Daniel's uneasiness

grew, fed by Caleb's. They had a quick breakfast and made their good-byes.

The ride home was a happy one as Mary Anna and Daniel exchanged information they had accrued about the West family.

"It's good to know friends are nearby," Daniel said, as pleased about the visit as Mary Anna.

Mary Anna smiled her agreement. "Virginia said she would come when my time comes." She tried to read Daniel's face and found the relief etched around his lips she expected to find. "Guess you'll have to stick to delivering colts for the mares," she teased.

"Hey, I could do it if I needed to."

"I know that, but I also see the relief on your face."

"Well, you may not be as easy as the mare," he said to provoke her.

"I would hope it was because you were more attached to me," she deftly parried.

eight

Mary Anna lived off the happiness of her visit with Virginia for several days. She hoped to see her again before the baby came. And she certainly hoped to see her when the baby was born.

She was spending more time making tiny red flannel garments and salvaging some of Columbus' things from the bottomless trunk. Virginia had laughed hard at Mary Anna's story of the red flannel. "Sounds just like a man," she had grinned knowingly.

Mary Anna was now sleeping a little later than Daniel in the mornings. He was kind to leave her and feed the stock, then come back and have breakfast with her. The air was becoming quite brisk, and the hot breakfasts she prepared were appreciated.

During breakfast, they made their plans for the day. Daniel made sure he knew where everyone would be at any given time. He had warned Otto, and also told him not to alarm Mary Anna. "Just be on your guard." Otto, too was growing tense by the absence of the Indians.

"It's jest too quiet," he complained.

Mary Anna was enjoying that quiet in the softness of her bed, dreaming of happy things, when in her dreams she heard Daniel shout something to Otto. She heard shots and angry whoops, and she awoke, not wanting to finish the dream. But when she sat up, she heard gunfire splitting the air. Daniel and Otto were down by the horses fighting off an Indian raid.

Mary Anna jumped out of bed and ran to the fireplace to get the other rifle. When she turned around, she saw that the door to the cabin was open.

Little Columbus was walking as fast as his chubby legs would let him toward his father. And a Comanche warrior was bearing down on him at full gallop.

"Dear God, help me!" screamed Mary Anna as she sprinted clumsily to the boy.

The Indian leaned from his horse and swooped the boy into the air. She grabbed desperately for the small body and succeeded in holding fast to Columbus' rounded middle. The sudden jerk caused the Indian to momentarily loosen his one-handed grip and Columbus fell from his grasp. The passing pony's flanks smashed into Mary Anna, and she and the child fell heavily to the ground.

A shot sounded and the Indian slumped across the neck of his pony, still in full gallop.

Mary Anna untangled herself from her skirts and pushed herself into a low run, clutching Columbus tightly with both arms. She slammed the cabin door and dropped the heavy timber across it, sobbing silently with relief. The Colt revolver was on the mantle. She grabbed it, never turning loose of the crying child, and crouched across from the door by the fireplace, ready to kill anyone who entered the door. The hand that held the gun wasn't steady, but it was determined. She could feel her heart leaping around in her chest. She was cornered and ready to defend herself and her two children, even if it meant killing someone else.

The whooping and gunfire stopped, and in the silence she heard Daniel pounding on the door.

"Let me in, Mary Anna! Are you and the baby all right? Let me in!"

"Daniel, we're okay," she shouted as she ran for the door. When she opened the door, she fell into his arms sobbing. "Oh, I was so scared!"

Daniel's face was strained and drawn. "Otto and I were out

at the horse pens when they hit." His eyes were still filled with fear. "They came in just the way he said, riding low, hanging off their horses. Nothing to shoot at. They got all the horses, Mary Anna, all of them. There was nothing we could do. They had us pinned down and—"

"It doesn't matter, Daniel. We're alive! Wait, where's Otto?"

"Right here, ma'am," he grinned as he came limping in. "They plum scairt me, but they didn't get me."

There was a brief moment of laughter as the thick fear dissipated.

The three adults stood motionless, stunned with the suddenness of the attack.

Daniel walked over to Mary Anna. "I saw what you did for our son, the way you rescued him." There was awe in his voice. "You're the bravest woman I ever saw."

She shuddered. "I didn't think. I just ran for him." She looked up into his eyes. "If he'd gotten Columbus, I think I might have died."

"Ma'am, I ain't never seen no one charge a Comanche barehanded afore." The respect in Otto's voice was reflected in his face. "You're such a little bit of a thang. I couldn't believe you jest ran out and grabbed the boy outten that Comanche's hands. Whooeee!" He shook his head.

Her fear easing, Mary Anna shook her finger at both of them. "You just remember that the next time I tell you to do something!"

After the grins faded, problems loomed large. "What are we going to do about the horses?" Daniel asked. His anger and color were returning. "Meat is one thing, but this can't be ignored. We're cleaned out." Bitterness turned his blue eyes a darker color.

"We kin borry a horse from the Wests and go report it to the sheriff. Mebbe they kin git a posse together and track 'em down."

"Oh, Daniel, the Wests! What if they got hit, too!"

"They may not have come out as well as we did," he agreed.

"There's only two ways to get there. Walk or ride an ox."

"We got ourselves two oxen. You kin ride over to the West's and I kin ride into town and talk to the sheriff. Iffen the Wests are all right, you kin borry a horse and meet me there." The two men looked at Mary Anna.

"I'll be fine. You do what you have to." With bravado she added, "If the Indians come back, I'll get out my broom and shoo them away."

Otto looked serious. "They won't be back, ma'am. They got what they wanted. It's horses they need, and they got 'em already. You'll be as safe as a gopher in a burrow."

Daniel looked to her for reassurance. "You'll be all right?"

"I'll be all right." Her eyes were very bright.

As Daniel rode down the road on the slow-moving ox, he grumbled to himself. "I could walk faster than this." But he knew the six miles would go faster on the plodding animal. He was humiliated at having to ride an ox. Humiliated by his enemies. They could even be watching now, laughing at him. Humiliation, fear, and anger came together. Daniel wanted to hit something. To smash something. He wanted something to grapple with, but here he was, riding to his new friend and neighbor on a poky ox.

Scalding tears burned their way down his cheeks. It didn't matter what Mary Anna said about God. God shouldn't have let the bad guys win. True, Columbus and the rest of them were all right, but all the hard work of building up the horse herd was wasted. *It isn't fair! They have no right to my animals! This is free land. They've got the reservation to take care of them. It isn't fair!* His hands tightened on the reins until the knuckles were white. One thing he knew for sure. *The Indians won't drive me from the place I've chosen. It's mine because I've worked for it.* And even the shame of sitting on top a wide-backed ox couldn't make him leave.

Daniel was deeply relieved to hear Caleb's dogs barking as Caleb came out the cabin door. He looked calm and then alarmed when he saw Daniel minus a horse.

"They hit us. Got all my horses," Daniel said as he slid off the ox.

"Guess we'll be next," Caleb said matter-of-factly.

Before he could ask, Virginia was out the door. "Is Mary Anna all right?" The fear in her eyes dimmed as Daniel nodded.

"Let's get us some good horses and go to town and report this to the sheriff," said Caleb.

"Otto is on his way," Daniel replied with a smile. "'Course, it may take him a while. He's on the other ox."

"I'll go to your place and stay with Mary Anna," Virginia said. She was gathering up her things and getting her young son ready before Daniel could say thank you.

When the men reached town, they could see a crowd of men standing in front of the court house. They found Otto and stood with him.

"Sheriff, this raidin' has got to stop!" shouted one man.

The crowd raised their voices in assent.

"You've got to do something about these varmints. It's not safe out here as long as they think they can get away with stealing anything they want from us," shouted another.

"Now just hold your horses," said Sheriff Maloney. "The chances of catching the ones that done it are slim to none. They're long gone by now." He was calm and tried to reason with the crowd, but he was also a man of the people.

"Sheriff, I'm Joseph Salmon. Those Comanches stole thirty-seven horses from me. I was talking to Otto Lammert. His boss, Daniel Thornton, was wiped out, too. I'm too old to ride now, but you young men had better take care of this problem. Right now they're stealing horses." He looked grim. "I don't want to think about what they might be doing next."

Sheriff Maloney stroked his huge curling mustache. "Anyone who wants to be in the posse, hold up your right hand so I can deputize you. You're official." In his heart he felt this was a waste of time, but maybe they would get lucky.

The men picked up the Indians' trail at Rocky Creek in Hamilton. Then they discovered how true Salmon's prediction had been. They found Mr. Bean and his black laborer killed by arrows. The men were shocked into silence at this sudden escalation from stealing to killing. Four men volunteered to stay behind and bury the bodies.

When they caught up with the posse again, the news was worse. "We found Johnson."

Chesley Turnbow paled. "I know him. Dead?" The men nodded. "Arrows?" Again they nodded.

"We buried him, too," they assured Turnbow.

The men rode on. The trail was getting farther and farther out, and they were not prepared to stay out for long. But before turning back, they found several of Mr. Salmon's horses dead. The brand was unmistakable.

It was agreed the Indians had indeed gotten away and the thirteen men rode back to Stephenville.

⋧

Mary Anna was completely drained from the terror of the past hour. She pulled Columbus up with her in bed and sang quietly so he would go to sleep, and then she fell into a much needed rest.

She was awakened by pain. *Oh, no. Not yet. It's too soon. Maybe I hurt my hip when I fell,* she thought hopefully. But the contractions began to be regular and harder.

I can do this, she reminded herself as she got out of bed and collected the things she would need if the contractions led to an early birth. And then there was a blessed sound, the rattling of wheels.

"Open up, Mary Anna. It's me, Virginia." When Mary Anna opened the door, Virginia swept in with Albert in tow. "You look a little peaked."

As Mary Anna bent slightly with a contraction, she said, "Albert, you take Columbus outside the cabin and play. Don't go far," she warned. "I don't want the Indians to get you."

Albert nodded and took Columbus by the hand.

"And now, missy, let's get you to bed."

The pain continued to crescendo, and at the top of it, Mary Anna felt the sudden emptying of her womb. She waited for the cry that never came. Virginia worked on the infant, rubbing him and blowing in his face. He was a tiny, tiny baby who needed the safety of his mother's womb to finish growing. Virginia worked diligently, but to no avail. Finally she wrapped him in a clean piece of cloth and laid him in Mary Anna's numb arms. "I'm sorry."

Mary Anna looked at the underdeveloped baby. He already had a little dark fuzz on his head and a tiny pink mouth. He looked for all the world as if he were asleep in her arms. Somewhere in her heart, a hot stone burned. It grew and grew, but there was no way to stop the heat and the size of it. The heat dried her tears before they could flow. Her eyes were like coals in the fireplace, red and smoldering.

"They took my baby from me. The Comanches took my baby. I saved Columbus, but they got this one." She ran her fingers over the baby's soft cheeks and hair, memorizing the features she would have recognized anywhere. "I made you some happy red clothes, little one. I was counting the days until you came. Columbus is looking for you. Your father was so excited. We were all waiting for you. But you came too early."

Virginia waited for the tears, but they didn't come. "Let me have him. You sleep for a while. I'll wake you when Daniel gets here." She gently took the baby from Mary Anna's embrace and laid him in the waiting cradle Columbus had outgrown. Then she sat in the rocker and silently cried for the mother who couldn't.

⋙

When Daniel rode up to his home, Virginia was waiting in the doorway. He knew something was wrong by the look on her face. "Mary Anna had her baby. A boy. It was born dead," she said simply.

Daniel slid off his borrowed horse. "Is she all right?"

"I'm worried about her. She hasn't cried."

"I'll take care of the coffin," Otto offered and rode off toward the barn.

Daniel walked slowly into the house, paused at the cradle, and walked to Mary Anna lying in bed. He sat down and gathered her in his arms. "He's beautiful. I'm sorry. I'm sorry I wasn't here for you."

Her smile was tired. "It's not your fault. You did what you had to do. It just happened." She couldn't tell him about the awful feelings she had and her anger at the Comanche who caused her baby to be born too soon. It was too raw and too powerful to turn loose in the small cabin.

The next day the child was laid to rest in the Texas soil. Mary Anna held onto Daniel and felt a part of her was being put down in that hole. She was no stranger to death—it was part of everyone's life. But this was her child.

Caleb read the short service. Daniel clenched his jaws in sorrow and anger as loving words were read from the Bible. Mary Anna carefully felt nothing as the promises meant to comfort washed over her. All she heard was the memory of horses' hooves pounding as she clutched Columbus and the thump from her hard fall when the pony's flanks knocked her down. Her mind echoed with Indians' screams, her own voice calling for God's help, and shots and more shots.

She could see Caleb's lips moving and she knew he was reading from the Bible, but the words couldn't penetrate the sounds in her head. As soon as she saw Caleb stop talking, she walked toward the cabin. Virginia walked with her, and Daniel stayed to help finish with the burial of his son. Mary Anna couldn't bear to see dirt being put on top of the child.

She sat down in the rocker and moved to and fro silently. Virginia prepared a simple meal.

"Do you remember the story in the Bible when Jesus sent His disciples out in the boat?" Mary Anna asked. "He walked on the water and Peter tried to go to Him. As long as he looked at Jesus and trusted Him, Peter stayed on top of the water. But there was that one moment when he looked at the water and his feet, and he doubted. Then he began to sink.

"I'm sinking, Virginia. We don't belong out here where bad things happen. I think maybe we should have stayed in Tennessee Colony. I wouldn't have lost my baby there. I stepped out in faith, just knowing we were supposed to come out here. Now I'm doubting it, and I'm sinking. I can't see the Master's face. It's too dark. All I can see is my feet going into the water. I can't see His face."

"Time is a funny thing," Virginia responded. "It gets bent around and some things seem to last forever when it's really only a short while. And other things seem to pass so quickly you never really get to feel them. Right now you're caught in that strange time. You're in the middle of the story. But the end of the story is yet to come. Jesus reached out His hand and took Peter's. He pulled him back up out of the water. Give it time. Feel the pain. Live through it and let it wash over you. When you've spent the anger and the pain, you'll begin to feel the Master's hand reach for you and pull you up out of the water. I know. I've been in the water, too."

Mary Anna remembered the little girl Virginia had so recently lost.

"I'm listening to you. The words will sink in eventually. Right now I can't seem to feel anything but hatred and anger." Her eyes burned, but still no tears came. "I wanted to change Daniel's mind about the Indians. I felt sorry for them. I admired them. Otto's wish for me not to change my mind isn't going to happen. I understand how Daniel feels now."

"It's all right for you to know how Daniel feels. The important thing is how you will feel when time passes. A human can't live with hatred in his heart. It'll poison his soul. It kills. Give yourself time." Virginia placed a comforting hand on Mary Anna's shoulder. "Just give yourself time."

nine

Daniel rode into Stephenville with Caleb to see if there was any chance of buying some horses. They stopped at the mercantile store to pick up supplies and listened to the latest gossip.

"We need a fort around here," said Mr. Turnbow. Fred Gentry and Dave Roberts nodded their heads in agreement.

"But we can't get any government troops to come stay in it," argued another man.

"But it could be a place of refuge, like if you got caught out in the open, you wouldn't have to ride all the way to town to be safe," argued another man. More heads nodded in agreement.

"It doesn't have to be big. Just strong and safe."

The idea was talked up around town and organized. With many men helping, the small fort was erected as an emergency shelter.

The trees were donning their fall wardrobes. The last of the garden was put away and the smokehouse was full of food for the winter. As the first cold snap blew in, Mary Anna began to feel some semblance of normalcy in her life. Columbus was a handful to keep up with, and Mary Anna had stopped putting wild flowers on the baby's grave each day. She had come to terms with death. The red flannel baby clothes had been stored away. Someday there would be another child. Never for a moment did she think to replace the baby, but she yearned for another child to hold and love.

Daniel, Caleb, and Otto built a strong barn for the winter. It had been an enormous undertaking, and when it was finished Daniel decided to have a celebration. Caleb was to bring

Virginia and Albert, and Otto asked a young woman he was courting in town.

Mary Anna got caught up in the gaiety. She cooked for two days, and when the day came, she spent a long while grooming herself for the party.

"You look like a bride," Daniel told her. Her eyes sparkled. "I haven't seen that joy in your eyes in a long while." He gathered her into his arms and danced her around the small cabin.

"Turn me loose! I've still a hundred things to do," she scolded him with a smile.

She had smoothed the dirt floor with her broom and washed the quilt on their bed. The table cloth was bright and cheerful, and she had polished the dishes with her dish cloth until she could see herself in them. She had done the best she could to make this a nice place. She was careful Daniel didn't see the frown on her face as she looked around the starkness of their home. For a fragment of a moment she wondered if it would always be like this, and then hurried on with her dream of having a beautiful home some day.

Hearing the rattle of wagon wheels, Mary Anna smoothed her dress and moved to answer the door. Virginia, Caleb, and Albert were the first to arrive, followed closely by Otto with his friend in a borrowed buggy.

"He must be serious about her if he borrowed a buggy," whispered Daniel. Mary Anna grinned. It would be nice to see young love in bloom.

Otto took off his hat. His cheeks were a high color and his grin self-conscious. "This here is Miss Angel Gilbert. Miz Thornton, Mr. Thornton, Mr. and Miz West."

"I'm pleased to meet you," Angel replied to their greetings. She was tall and slender with curly, brown-gold hair pulled back modestly into a soft bun. Some of the curls had escaped her comb and fluffed over her oval face in a most becoming way. She seemed perfectly at ease. The only thing that gave her away was her cold hands.

Food was brought in from the outside and added to the spread Mary Anna had prepared.

"Don't stand on ceremony," Daniel instructed them. "Dig in. Dig in."

"Miss Gilbert doesn't eat much, does she?" Daniel whispered to Mary Anna.

"No young girl is going to eat much when her beau is watching, no matter how hungry she is. It isn't ladylike."

"So that's why you picked at your food when I was courting and now I can't fill you up," he teased.

Otto and Angel were sitting close together on a split log bench, doing more talking than eating. She was hanging onto his every word, and Mary Anna could see how important it made him feel. *She'll have him roped and tied in no time,* she thought, and she grinned at Daniel who was also watching the tableau. Miss Angel was careful to touch Otto's arm often and gaze into his eyes with big saucers of her own. Her laugh was pleasant, and each time it gurgled, Otto's chest got a little larger.

As Mary Anna listened to them talk, she was reminded of that day on the quilt when she and Daniel had exchanged dreams. *She has the same dreams I had when I came here,* she thought with a start. *She's only seventeen, three years younger than I am.* But Mary Anna felt much, much older as she listened to the girl's prattle. She smiled up at her husband. "Do you suppose that's the way I sounded when I talked to my stepmother before we were married?"

"Were we really ever that young?" Daniel countered.

With the three couples together, everything seemed funnier and the food tasted better. They were good friends gathered together to celebrate.

"Daniel, get out that fiddle of yours. I'm pining to be dancing with my wife," called Caleb.

Out under a checkered picnic cloth of stars, they spun and

wheeled as Daniel's fiddle spun melodic magic and made the gingham skirts whirl.

The courtship going on lent a delicious flirtatiousness to the married couples. They forgot the hardships and remembered the beginning of their own romances. For a while each couple seemed wrapped up in their own world of memories, and mouths hardened by life softened with new smiles.

Caleb spelled Daniel with his mouth harp and Mary Anna found herself in Daniel's arms waltzing to the sweet strains of "Aura Lee." *How tall and handsome Daniel is,* she noted with pride. *Probably the best looking man here.* She felt his lean body moving to the music, and the cold stone buried deep inside her flaked off one chip. *Concentrate on what you have today and forget about yesterday. Let it go. Keep your eyes on the Master.* She lay her head down on Daniel's broad chest and gave herself up to the rhythm and the movement of the moment.

⊰⊱

The September wind had a decided bite to it as Mary Anna struggled back up from the stream with the heavy bucket of fresh water. Short of hiking up her skirts, there was no way to keep them dry, and they dragged around her ankles, making the task harder. Soon the relatively easy task of getting water to the cabin was going to be a miserable chore.

Daniel had been pleased to feel the air. "The cotton bolls will pop open," he promised.

Then all of them would share in the back-breaking job of picking the fluffy white fiber for Mary Anna to make cloth and then new clothing during the cold winter months when they were cabin-bound.

She was fairly certain she carried another child for a June delivery. A smile crept around her mouth as she remembered the red flannel clothes waiting in the trunk.

The men were out planting peach trees for an orchard. The

thought of ripe peaches made her mouth water. *One day I'll be putting up preserves and baking peach cobblers.* Patience was one virtue all pioneer women were forced to practice unendingly. Everything they did took a long time to finally enjoy. *From babies to peaches,* she mused.

Soldier, now a leggy adolescent, had monitored her trip to the spring and now lay down in his hole by the cabin door. He had reached his full size, though he would add a few pounds.

Mary Anna gathered a few scraps and tossed them to him. As he gulped the food impolitely, she stroked his black and white coat. His long tail beat the air in pleasure.

Columbus came steadily out the door, plopping down beside the hound. His curly hair hung in ringlets around his chubby face.

"Careful now. Pat him softly," Mary Anna instructed as he tried to grab a handful of hair from Soldier's back. The dog licked her hand, getting the last traces of crumbs from her fingers.

Mary Anna left them and went into the cabin. It was bread day, and she looked forward to getting her hands into the fragrant dough.

She had just put the first batch into the fire to bake when she heard Soldier's low warning growl. She shaded her eyes and saw a band of Indians on the horizon. Soldier was in a guardian stance as they watched the Indians move away from them.

Mary Anna's pounding heart settled a bit, and she took her hand from the gun on the shelf by the door. A good deal of the sorrow she had felt for Indians had died with her baby.

At noon Daniel and Otto came in from the fields, hot and dirty. "Got the peach trees in and the cotton hoed," Daniel said. "Shouldn't be long now 'til we can pick it."

"I saw a band of Indians a while ago." Mary Anna put the hot stew and fresh bread in front of them.

"We did, too. It was a mixed band, not a raiding party," he

added reassuringly. He took a bite of stew and chewed it carefully. "Robert Wylie and I are going to take some cattle to Palo Pinto tomorrow."

She wanted to argue with him, to ask him to wait a day or two, as though that would make some difference, but she knew it would be useless. Raising cattle and horses was their primary reason for being here.

"I need some cash money and this is a fast way to get it," he continued. "You'll have Soldier and Otto to protect you."

They exchanged steady gazes.

"We'll be fine," she said a little too brightly. "It's you I worry about."

"Wylie has been to Palo Pinto before. We should only be gone a few days. We don't have a big herd to move, but we have to do it before the winter sets in." He took a bit of bread. "I'll stop by town and pick up a few things. Can't bring much by horse, though. Make me a desperate list." He tried to get her to grin.

She made the effort and then enumerated the critical list and said no more. Uneasiness made her mute.

When Daniel left the following day, Mary Anna hugged him tightly. "God's speed," was all she said. But she prayed for him off and on throughout the day and was more alert than usual to everything around her.

"Lord, I know I've been mad at you about the baby. And my heart has hardened against the Indians, but please take care of Daniel in spite of my sins."

ð

Being on the trail again feels good, Daniel thought as he began the drive. It was a welcome break from his steady chores at home. Rocking in the saddle of a good horse, new sights, and a feeling of adventure made him feel keenly alive.

Beyond the dust his small herd kicked up, Daniel could see another sandy cloud, and he pushed his cows toward it. There was always a risk it was Indians, but the cloud stood over the rendezvous spot he had agreed on with Wylie. He loosened his rifle and pulled it across the saddle horn, just in case. Then he saw the familiar roan Wylie rode and Wylie himself waving his hat high in the air.

They had to work hard to mix the two herds of cows. Cows are like some people, they don't accept newcomers. So it was a skittish group the men tried to move.

The men alternated the dirty job of riding the dusty drag and the relative pleasant point. Even so, Daniel's white shirt was the color of the red trail dust in no time at all. And in spite of the neckerchief he wore over his mouth, he had eaten a pound of dirt.

They pushed the cattle hard and fast, getting them away from their home range as quickly as possible. "Don't give 'em time to think" was one of the first axioms of herding.

They had only been out about an hour when Daniel saw another cloud of dust on the horizon. The chances of it being another herd were slim, and as he began to make out the riders, his worst fears were realized.

Daniel waved his hat in the air and shouted to Wylie, "The fort!"

The Indian raiding party was bearing down on them at full gallop.

Daniel raised his rifle over the head of the cattle and fired, starting the herd into a mad run. Using his horse to loosely point the leaders toward the fort, he hoped his mount wouldn't stumble and throw him under the pounding hooves.

The fort was close by and soon part of the band gave up the chase, but Daniel saw three braves riding low and fast toward the remuda. The remuda was made up of Wylie's horses, but Daniel was determined the Comanches wouldn't get them. Fury rose like a gorge in his throat and he reined his horse to a stop, knelt down, and took careful aim at the marauding men. His first shot was too high.

Take your time. Easy now. He squinted down the barrel and squeezed off another shot. The man dropped from his horse. The herd was racing past him, their dust choking his eyesight. He quickly wiped his eyes and pulled the trigger again. He missed, but the other two Indians turned their ponies and made a pass at their downed comrade, swooping him from the ground between them. One man skillfully maneuvered the body in front of him, and the would-be cattle thieves rode away, sitting high once they were out of Daniel's range of fire.

The cattle were milled to a walk outside the fort and then driven inside.

Wylie had a big grin on his face as he came alongside Daniel's horse. "Good shooting there."

Daniel's anger had subsided, but his heart was still racing. "Maybe next time we ought to take a couple more men with us, Wylie. I'd like the odds better," he said wryly.

"Seemed like a good idea at the beginning. Ain't had any raids in a while. But we'll scare us up a couple of good pokes before we set out again."

"Want me to go back to town for them?"

Wylie grinned slowly. "The way you fight Injuns, you're sure to get there. I'll jest wait here. Try the mercantile store. There's usually either someone hanging out there or someone who knows where to look." He stepped down off his horse and knocked some of the dust out of his well-worn hat. "At least we won't have to ride drag no more. Low man on the totem pole gets the drag. And we're the bosses." His smile grew larger at the thought.

When Daniel returned to the fort, he had two men with him. Wylie stuck out his hand as they introduced themselves.

"MacDougle's the name," said the huge, red-haired, bearded bear of a man. His Scottish burr gave away his homeland.

"Snake." The man looked like a Baptist deacon, dressed in

black with a large black hat. His hair was a thin blond and blew in the wind unrepressed as he took off his hat and shook hands. "Kind of a small herd. How far you going?"

"Palo Pinto to join up with another herd," said Wylie.

"They're likely to be hiring on for the drive to the rail head," said MacDougle. "Beautiful country, America. Texas has been my favorite by far, though."

Daniel was curious about why a Scotchman was in Texas, but it was taboo to ask a man about his past. Everyone came to Texas with a clean slate. His actions from then on would make his reputation. At the end of the drive, Daniel would know no more about the man than he did this day, for he never spoke of the past.

Wylie was the talker of the bunch. He told hair-raising stories at the campfire of his growing up days with eight brothers. And there were the ever-present card games. No cowboy worth his salt would say no to a card game after supper. They bet smooth river stones and played as hard for them as if they were gold pieces.

They took turns with the night watch, but there was no more trouble with the Indians. All four men looked calm, but a sudden noise in the night could cause even the deepest sleeper to rear up with his gun in his hand.

"Don't shoot! It's me, Snake!" called a frightened voice as he returned from a trip to the bushes to find three guns pointed at him from the rim of the firelight.

Mumbled grumblings of relief sounded as the men settled down again.

Daniel squirmed around, trying to make his neck more comfortable on the saddle. Riding in the saddle had been wonderful at first, but as he used it for an uncomfortable pillow, Daniel was sure the saddle would make both ends of his body sore by morning. For a brief moment he wished he was in his soft bed with Mary Anna. *This isn't as much fun as I remembered,* he thought as he drifted to a light sleep.

The days were filled with dirt and tension, and the nights with sore muscles and more tension. The only time Daniel relaxed was when Wylie was telling one of his improbable stories about his family around the campfire after supper.

"Yes, siree," Wylie said, "we bet my little brother he couldn't git his mouth around that brass door knob. Mama was plumb sore at us when he did. And then there was the time we told him to put his tongue on the wagon wheel. 'Course it was about twenty below freezin' at the time." He laughed at his memory.

"Never heard a kid yell so loud withoutten him being able to use his tongue. Now this time it was Daddy that took exception to our funnin'. I don't think any of us boys sat down for near to a week after he took us to the woodshed." He took a deep breath. "Spent a lot of time in that there woodshed," he finished. "Miss my brothers, too." He didn't offer to tell what had happened to them, and no one asked. Each man took the time to miss his own family rather than question Wylie about his.

They finally met up with the other herd and business was concluded. Snake and MacDougle signed on with the herd as they had planned. Wylie and Daniel turned their horses back the way they had come.

As the two men started out for home, the skies rumbled over them and darkened. They brought out the slickers and pulled their hats down lower. The first day's ride was a long, wet one.

That night they made a rude shelter from a tarp and a smokey fire.

"Sure is a glamorous way to make a living, ain't it?" Wylie said as he wrung out his wet socks.

"Says so in all the pulps," Daniel replied. He looked out over the wet range land where an ashen white moon was struggling with the threads of the storm clouds for room. "Not glamorous, maybe, but it's real." He leaned against the tree they had strung the tarp from and said, "I'd rather be out here right now than sittin' in some fine office in fancy clothes."

His blue eyes shone in the firelight. "Out here I can touch and hear what I'm working for. I have a goal and each day I can measure how close I am to it." He laughed. "'Course some days it seems to gallop away from me."

Wylie laughed with him. "I know what you're sayin'. Men have said it in fancy ways, but I understand. Out here we take life by the throat and shake out a living, make it give us the dream."

And that night Daniel slept with a big wad of that dream under his saddle. That money would see him through the winter months. Until he could do it again. And next time it would be a bigger herd.

When at last he held Mary Anna in his arms and tossed a squealing Columbus into the air, he drew his first easy breath.

"How was the drive?" she asked.

"Hard work. But I got my cash money." He reached inside his swinging leather vest. "And I got my best girl some peppermint."

She laid her head on his dirty white shirt and hugged him more tightly.

"Oh, and I found some material that'll better suit your needs for making clothes for the new baby," he grinned.

He shook hands with Otto. "Thanks for being here. It sure took a load off my mind."

❧

As winter closed in on them, Mary Anna was not hard pressed to find things to do. She spent hours picking the cotton seeds out of the fluff and carding the fiber to make thread. For days the hum of her spinning wheel was the music to which she worked. Then she wove the thread on her loom into soft cloth and replaced their worn summer things and added to their winter wardrobe.

There was still the cooking to do and Columbus to keep up with and the laundry that never seemed to end. But she felt energetic, and her pregnancy didn't slow her down.

She still tended the grave occasionally on a fair day, but with the prospect of another baby, her deep grief eased.

Lord, I can feel Your healing hands helping me to walk across the water to the boat, and for that I thank You, she prayed as she walked away from the little grave site.

The weather grew steadily colder and Daniel recaulked their cabin. There was a good stack of firewood by the back door and Mary Anna hung her extra quilts over the walls by their beds. They looked cheerful and they kept the cabin warmer.

Warmer was what they would need as the thermometer steadily dropped.

Daniel and Otto were wrapped up in many layers of clothing as they tended the animals. Even so, their faces were red with the cold as they came stomping into the cabin.

"I don't like it, Otto. I think the bottom is going to drop out tonight. It's too blue over in the west." Both men took off their work gloves and hats, shucked off their heavy coats, and hung them on the pegs by the door.

"Yup, sure as shootin' it's gonna freeze hard tonight," he agreed. "But we've done what we could for the animals. They should be all right."

"Got a hearty, bone-warming supper for you two," Mary Anna said as she rose from her rocker by the fire.

The men dug in to the thick meat pies, and Mary Anna asked innocently, "Is there going to be a wedding anytime soon, Otto?"

Otto's spoon stopped in mid air. He looked guilty as a boy caught with his hand in the cookie jar. "Why, ma'am, I'm not sure."

"You have asked her, haven't you?" Mary Anna grilled him.

Otto dropped his eyes and laid his spoon down carefully by

his plate. "Now, ma'am, I have wrote out several things I'd like to say to Angel, I mean Miss Gilbert, but none of them seems to be just the thing I'd really like to say to her."

Mary Anna settled down in her rocker again and took up her sewing. "Just what would you like to say to her?"

Otto turned positively scarlet. He was caught. He couldn't be impolite to Mary Anna, and there was no way in the world he could tell her what he'd like to say to Angel. He took a big bite of food and chewed thoughtfully. Mary Anna waited him out.

He was about to take another huge bite when she said, "Well, Otto?" The shadows hid the amusement on Mary Anna's face.

Otto sputtered a bit and then stammered and added a few hems and haws.

"Mary Anna, have pity on this boy," Daniel pleaded. "You don't need to know what he and Miss Gilbert are planning or are not planning."

Otto sighed in relief, sure he was off the hook.

"But I do! I'm the one who will have to look at his miserably sad face if she says no or put up with the silly grin and half-brained job he'll do if she says yes. I need to get myself ready for either event."

Otto opened his mouth to respond, but nothing came out, and he closed it thoughtfully.

Daniel jumped in. "I would need to know so I could get the chivaree organized. And of course, you'll probably bake the wedding cake as a gift to the bride and groom," he added hesitantly. "And there's the parson to get hold of. Lord only knows where he's at on the circuit right now."

"And it will take months to get a proper wedding dress made. She probably already has a good hope chest started, but they will need a place to live. Do you think you should build a cabin out here close to us, or will you live in town close to her parents?" Mary Anna was having a hard time stifling her laughter as she saw the panic grow on Otto's face.

"Which do you think you'll do, Otto?" asked Daniel innocently.

"I, I, I think I'll check the stock one more time," mumbled a frantic Otto as he rose and grabbed his hat and coat. He exited to gales of smothered laughter.

"He may not show up 'til next spring, Mary Anna. Your foolishness may have cost me a good hand," laughed Daniel.

"And you didn't help, did you?" she retorted.

Almost as soon as the door shut firmly, it opened again. It was Otto, but there was no merriment or embarrassment on his face.

"Mr. Thornton, Indian family here." He wasn't frightened, so Daniel took time to put on his coat and casually reach for his rifle. As he stepped through the door, Mary Anna put on her heavy shawl and stood in the slightly opened door to watch.

It was the same young family that had come to them in the spring. The young, blue-eyed girl was swathed in a buffalo hide blanket against the bitter cold. Mary Anna could just distinguish the lump of her baby inside the robe against her. The young warrior was haughty as he asked for food for his family. They were a pitiful sight. Proud and hungry. A once mighty nation fallen and asking for crumbs from their enemy's table.

Daniel turned to come back in to the cabin. Mary Anna wasn't sure if it was to get food or to leave them there in their misery. But his eyes saw the great mercy in hers and he barked to Otto, "Get them some meat and potatoes." Then he pushed past Mary Anna and entered his own warm home to finish his nurturing supper.

"Thank you," Mary Anna told her tight-lipped husband as he firmly closed the door.

Gruffly he replied, "Better to give them a few things than to have them steal a whole cow from us."

Mary Anna wasn't sure if he was being practical or had shown a kindness to the people he hated, but she was satisfied he had fed them.

His kindness was not rewarded, for that night a cow disappeared. Daniel ranted and raged against the Indians, swearing never to help them again. That night an ice storm blew in and killed a few more cattle and probably many of the baby peach trees they had so carefully planted.

Daniel was unrepentant. "I'm not going to feed even one more family. It does no good. And if that makes the Lord mad at me, so be it."

Mary Anna said, "Daniel, it makes me go cold all over to hear you speak like that!"

"What's made you cold is the weather." And he stomped out to the pens to work out his anger.

"Forgive him, Lord. He doesn't mean to be disrespectful to You," Mary Anna prayed. "Help his heart to soften a little and his tongue a lot."

ten

As February doggedly locked her harsh wintery arms around the earth, Mary Anna began dreaming of the warm spring. She hated the long winters and suffered in the frigid temperatures. Her feet were never warm, and her hands were chapped almost to the point of bleeding, no matter how much she tried to protect them.

March followed its normal course and came in angry and growly. They had a small party for Columbus' birthday, and Mary Anna made little honey cakes with the precious little sugar they had left. Provisions were growing slim in spite of their careful stockpiling. She knew it wouldn't be long until Daniel would have to leave for more supplies. Or send Otto.

Mary Anna could feel spring coming. She imagined she could smell roses from the garden back home. Little by little, winter began to lose ground to the insistent sun, and the days began to hold the promise of warmth.

Mary Anna's spirits rose with the temperature. She yearned to feel the rich soil of her garden. She began to go outdoors again and revel in the sweetness of the still-cool air.

Daniel made his trip to town for provisions uneventfully, and Mary Anna was able to relax with Otto and Soldier for protection. But she didn't forget to ask the Lord for His guardianship for all of them.

Daniel brought back all the news of the town. Virginia West had borne a girl. His smile was lazy as he added, "But we'll have the first boy born in Erath county."

"How can you be so sure?" she challenged.

"Oh, I just know this time," he said smugly.

April's rain washed away the last of winter and the whole earth seemed to open its eyes at once. Mary Anna felt dizzy with relief. *We made it through our first winter,* she exalted.

Thomas Peter, to be called Peter, was born at the end of May. He was healthy and his cry hearty as Mary Anna proudly showed him off to Daniel, Columbus, and Otto. Virginia shooed them out the door and finished caring for mother and child.

"It's such a comfort to have you here, Virginia. A good midwife is more valuable than gold."

"I know that, for I had one to help me." She sat on the edge of the bed, smoothing the covers as she talked. "I never considered medical care such a precious thing until I didn't have any out here." She looked sad. "Maybe a doctor could have saved my little girl. Maybe not. But having someone with you in a crisis is, well, no one should ever have to be alone and go through serious illnesses."

She looked Mary Anna in the eyes squarely. "You are a healer. You aren't using your talent fully yet, but you have it. The time will come when you will be valued and loved for your very presence," she said softly. She took Mary Anna's hands in her own. "Yes, you have a talent for doctoring. And you will use it well and wisely."

Mary Anna felt protests begin to rise in her throat, but her heart heard the words, and they touched a resonance of perfect harmony.

Virginia saw her words had been accepted and said, "Well, now I'll get some supper fixed for those young men out there while you care for Peter. He's a fine boy." She beamed with the joy of having helped bring the tiny being into the world.

Mary Anna smiled too. The spring of 1858 was starting off with great joy and expectations for the young Thornton family.

❧

Mary Anna was working in her herb garden. She knew she would be needing an extensive one. Virginia's words had opened her eyes to a calling she felt deep inside, and she was preparing herself to be helpful whenever she could. She knew a lot about herbs from Louisa, and one of the books she had brought with her at her stepmother's insistence was a book on herbal healing.

She glanced up every now and then to check on the baby sleeping in his basket close by. Four-year-old Columbus was playing with Soldier, throwing a stick for the dog to retrieve. Mary Anna had her new rifle propped against the rude fence that surrounded the spacious garden. They were still having trouble with the Indians, and she was ever mindful of danger. Daniel and Otto were plowing the fields, and she could see the little puffs of dust behind the plow float up into the soft spring sky.

The sun made her long-sleeved dress and poke bonnet warm to work in, and the cotton gloves on her hands were damp with perspiration where she held the hoe. Carefully she worked the rich soil around the tender plants until she heard the steady pound of horses' hooves coming up the rough road. Shading her eyes, she recognized Caleb, and he was riding hard, a sure sign of trouble. He headed straight for the men and then Daniel came to her with the news.

His face was set hard as granite. "The Lemley girls have been kidnapped by the Comanches," he said without preliminaries.

"Oh, no!" she gasped.

"We're going to try to get them back."

There was no point in exploring the possibilities of what might happen to the two girls if they weren't rescued. Mary Anna was torn between her fear for the children and the terror the parents were going through.

She watched the men ride away from her and silently prayed for all the people involved in this ordeal. Then she spent her energy on the plants and her thoughts of why the Indians did what they did.

"Lord, I can understand the Indians fighting with the settlers to keep their land, but I don't understand the cruelty of
their revenges. Why can't someone sit down and work this
out? It could all be so simple. We get this land, and they get
that land, and everyone should be happy. Why does it have to
include the children? I've heard what they do to the children.
And to the women they steal. Lord, why can't this be settled
between the men? I don't understand. Oh, please, dear Lord,
keep those little girls safe and let Daniel and the men find
them quickly to bring them home to those who love them.
Please." Tears filled her eyes. Her heart tore as if it had been
her boys taken away.

Then fear struck. Was she being watched right now? With
fear pulling at her, she grabbed the children and ran for the
cabin. Columbus was very unhappy at being inside on such a
nice day, and she was hard pressed to keep him occupied. She
was jumpy, and Columbus' irritability plucked at her tightly
strung nerves.

Daniel and Otto didn't come home for dinner, but then she
didn't know when to expect them. She sat in the rocker with a
small fire in the fireplace to mend by until her eyes were ach-
ing with fatigue. There was no question of sleeping until Daniel
and Otto returned.

It was close to dawn when they returned, haggard and saddle
weary. She peeped out cautiously before she opened the door
all the way. Daniel's grin was weary, but victorious.

"You got them! Are they all right? Were they hurt? Poor
babies, they must have been scared to death. Oh, Daniel, talk
to me!"

"I'm just waiting until you take a breath." He smiled and
hugged her at the same time. "Yes, they were scared, but they're
fine and back home." He sighed. "We followed the Indians to a
camp and waited until they were bedded down. We stampeded

their horses and cut them down."

"You killed them?"

"I don't think they would have been willing to just hand the girls over to us," he said wryly.

She wanted to say, "You could have tried to trade for them," but bit her tongue. She hadn't been there, so she couldn't know what it had been like. Maybe they had done the only thing they could. She looked carefully at his face and saw nothing. Daniel was numb. His eyes held a haunted look and his color was ashen. She wanted to ask if killing those men would mean more retaliations by the Indians on the settlers. Instead she said, "Come and I'll feed you."

"Too tired to eat. I just want to go to bed." Daniel knew nothing would stay in his stomach. The sights and sounds and smells of the killing had sickened him. Indian or white man, death like that was ugly, and he hated being a part of it. He tried to tell himself it was like killing a rabid animal to put it out of its misery and keep other people safe, but he wasn't sure he could accept that measurement of human life.

Mary Anna noted a similar look on Otto's face as he headed into his sleeping room.

She lay next to the person she loved most in the world, wondering if she would ever really know him. With this incident, had God begun to change Daniel's hatred of Indians? *Please, God, take away the hate and replace it with a desire for peace.*

❧

Daniel knew full well what the Indians might do in retaliation for rescue of the Lemley girls. He and Otto were more vigilant than ever. News had come in the way of a passing stranger. He wouldn't talk in front of Mary Anna, but as he and Daniel and Otto sat outside under the tree, he had warned them.

The stranger's story made Daniel think of the stories he and his brothers had told under the covers at the plantation when they had wanted to scare each other to death. But this was real.

And he was here with his family.

The man's story dripped with the blood of innocents murdered and mutilated by the renegade Indians. He spoke in low tones that added to the horror. He said names like Nocona, the Comanche chief, and Geronimo, the Apache warrior. And then he said the most horrible thing of all. "You do realize that you are sittin' smack dab in the middle of one of the Comanche war trails down into Mexico, don't ya?"

Daniel's hair rose in a prickle from his scalp and his heart skipped a beat. "Yes." Yes, he knew, but he hoped it wasn't true.

"Yup." The stranger wiped his dirty face with an equally filthy hand. "The gov'ment ain't gonna be no help either. There's too much land for the few men they have. Gonna have to be some changes made iffen they expect white folks to stay out here on the frontier." He saw the fear in Daniel's eyes and said, "Don't worry. I won't say anything to the little lady." Then he looked at Daniel again. "I'd dare to say she knows she ain't in civilization, but there's no need to scare her to death."

Daniel nodded his thanks and looked at Otto. The younger man was white as the moonlight, and his eyes were as frightened as Daniel's.

"We've had our run-ins with the Indians, Comanches mostly." He told the story of the Lemley girls.

"You know you're a marked man," the stranger said flatly. "They'll never forgive nor forget you." He sighed deeply. "If I wuz you, I'd pack up right now and move back aways. At least close to a big fort. There's time enough for you to make your fortune after things are settled with the Indians."

Something inside Daniel recoiled at those words. "I didn't come out here to do things the easy way. I came out here to make something of this land. I can make something productive out of it. More and more whites are moving in. We'll take care of ourselves."

Even in the moonlight, the stranger and Otto could see Daniel's resolve. The strong planes of his face were set hard. The stranger shrugged and tapped out the ashes of his pipe. "I'll be pleased to sleep in your barn tonight. That straw sounds mighty soft. I'll be going at first light."

That night as he lay beside Mary Anna, Daniel had his first serious inspection of his thoughts on God since coming to Erath county. *Does God care what happens to me and mine? Or did He just start the world and now He sits back and watches? People say miracles happen, but I'm not sure if they're miracles by God or extraordinary good luck. Why would God let people like the Indians exist? How can He let them do such terrible things to other human beings and not wipe them out with His power—if He has so much?*

Logic chased reason and knowledge from his childhood around in his head. The things he knew about religion didn't fit out here in the frontier. Long ago he had ceased to depend on God for anything in his life. Now didn't seem to be a fitting time to begin again. Stubbornly he thought, *I'm not going to turn to God in fear. I don't want that kind of God. Mary Anna can do the praying for both of us.* And he turned over and fell into a restless sleep.

❧

Mary Anna was serving Daniel his breakfast when she casually asked, "What did the stranger say about the Indians? Any retaliations because of the Lemley girls?"

Daniel knew better than to lie to her. "Some. We're well warned and armed. Just be a little more careful than usual." His voice was level, but for Mary Anna it held a world of frightening information.

Soldier gave a low growl and ran to the door barking. Daniel was quick to get his gun and hurry to the door. When he opened it, the rattling of a wagon could be clearly heard. Shouts of, "Hello!" and "Look at the house!" drifted in. Then came those sweet words: "Mary Anna, it's us! We're here!"

Mary Anna grabbed her shawl and almost got it around her before she hit the cold ground in a dead run. "Papa! Louisa! I can't believe it! It must be a dream!" And then everyone was hugging everyone.

"Jacob, you've grown a foot since I last saw you," Mary Anna exclaimed to her oldest brother. And to each of her four other siblings she made similar remarks, but the one who had changed the very most was baby Vera. "How pretty you are, and so grown up! Give me a big hug!" Baby Vera's little curls danced up and down excitedly as she reached for her big sister. "I'm not a baby anymore," she said in a six-year-old voice.

"Of course, you're not. Oh, you and Columbus will have such a good time playing together. And you can help take care of little Peter." Vera's face shone with grown-up joy at the thought.

"Well, come on in and let's get all of you fed." There was a lot of talking and laughter as the food was passed around and gratefully consumed. As she saw that each one was cared for, Mary Anna asked a million questions and got a million in return.

Peter Garland sat in Daniel's chair and happily ate the venison offered. Louisa sat in Mary Anna's chair, thoroughly enjoying a hot cup of coffee laced heavily with cream. Peter wiped his mouth carefully on his sleeve and said, "You haven't lost your touch, girl."

Mary Anna still felt she was in the middle of a dream.

"You look plum surprised, darlin'." He was delighted he had caused such a stir. "We got tired of the soft life at the hotel, and decided to have an adventure, like you."

"Humpt! He decided, not me." Louisa took a spoonful of hominy and then added, "I'd have rather stayed in the soft life." But her face gentled as she said to Mary Anna, "You're looking well. Pioneer life hasn't hurt you. You look older, but somehow more handsome." She smiled. "And two fine sons!"

She saw the look of pride as well as the knife edge of pain in Mary Anna's eyes. She knew that look, the look of a dead child. Later she would find out about it.

"Tell us your plans, and Otto and me will help you get settled out here," Daniel offered. Otto gave them a shy smile of assent. He looked completely at home among the Thornton clan.

"I guess it's simple arithmetic. The more white people there are, the fewer Indians that can stay around. We're here to help settle this part of Texas. The land is beautiful. Soon Stephenville will be needing a good hotel, and we just happen to be in the hotel business." He smiled benevolently.

"From the news I've been hearing, you might not have anybody to rent those rooms to," Louisa said tartly. "Is it true the army is gone? That scares the Irish out of me."

Daniel answered her honestly. "Yes, most of them are gone. And the Indians are riled up because we rescued the Lemley girls. Things are a bit frightening right now."

"We heard about it in town," Peter replied soberly. "I guess our arrival is a timely one. We can help keep watch until this thing has settled down."

"It isn't going to be settled down until all the Indians are on a reservation," Daniel said flatly.

Mary Anna and Louisa exchanged looks of mutual concern.

"But they are on a reservation. Most of them, anyway," Mary Anna said reasonably.

"They aren't staying there," Daniel argued. "If they did, we wouldn't be having all this trouble."

Mary Anna bit her tongue and said carefully, "If they were getting what they needed, they wouldn't come to our door and beg for meat."

Peter and Louisa exchanged covert looks as the marital discord hung in the air. "No matter," said Peter, "we've come to be together as a family again. Now, lass, come outside and see what we've brought you." The tension melted in the warmth of wonderful gifts: spices, pieces of lace, and for Columbus, a metal monkey that clanged cymbals together when he was wound up.

The evening was festive and full of remembrances. When it was time to bed everyone, there was a very short discussion about the two older boys sleeping in the barn. "We can't chance it, boys," Daniel said. "If the Indians raid us, you'd be off by yourselves."

Otto added casually. "Why, I'm even going to sleep here in the cabin. If trouble comes, we all want to be together to help." That settled any discussion. When all were bedded down wall to wall on pallets, Daniel kissed Mary Anna good night quietly in their bed.

"I'm sorry I lost my temper," he whispered.

"I'm sorry, too," she said as she snuggled closer to him in the faded light of the banked fire. She wanted to say more. To tell him there had to be an answer to all the killing and raiding and hating. But there were too many people in the cabin to have a heart-to-heart talk, so she snuggled close to him and held her peace.

Lord, keep us safe tonight, and thank You for bringing my family together again. Help us to see the Indians as Your children, too. Please, let there be peace among us. And help Daniel to come to love You as I do, for I'm sure then he will see the Indians as human beings, too.

She gave a tiny grin as she felt another piece of the stone in her heart flake off. Virginia was right. Time was a great healer. It gave her a fairer perspective. Virginia's promise that Mary Anna was a healer flitted through her mind. *Physician, first heal thyself.* And she drifted off to sleep hearing the gentle snoring of her family and feeling a cabinful of love.

❧

Awful screams and loud cries of horses woke Mary Anna as

the sunlight struggled to filter through the tiny chinks of the cabin walls. The shrill battle cries of the Comanches made the hair rise on her arms. Terror cramped her heart, and she couldn't pull any air into her lungs.

Daniel was already springing for his pants and his guns, hopping over sleeping bodies that were beginning to sit up in the din. "Indians!" he shouted, "Get your guns! Everybody stay down! Otto! Peter!"

There was no need to call Peter's name. The old military man was clutching his rifle, heading for the one shuttered window in the cabin. It had gun ports in it, and he peered out into the cold, misty half-light. A cry of dismay slipped through his lips as he saw the raiding band emptying the horses out of the corral and killing the cows randomly. In all his military years he had never seen such a sight as the magnificent horsemen wheeling and charging. Even in his fear he could appreciate the riding skills of the Comanche. He searched for a target and fired. He grunted with satisfaction as a man fell, and then gasped in astonishment as two other riders came in and picked up the wounded man between them.

Daniel was shooting through the gunport in the door. His mouth was dry with fear at the sight of the men. *There's never been so many before,* he thought. And then tears stung his eyes as he saw the first of the flames begin to lick at the corral that had been built with so much hard labor.

But as he saw those flames, fear knotted his stomach. He fired like a wild man trying to keep the raiders from getting close to the cabin. *Dear God, don't let them burn us out! Help us!* The prayer was said without a thought for theology. Instinctively he turned to the only One he knew that had the power to keep them alive. The God of his childhood. He felt they had a good chance of withstanding the firepower and arrows of the Indians, but there was not a chance in a thousand of them surviving without the safety of the cabin.

Mary Anna tried to calm the children and reload Daniel's rifle as quickly as he emptied it. The acrid smell of gunpowder, the ear-splitting noise of the guns, the screams of the terrified children, all made up the cacophony overpowering the small confines of the cabin.

Louisa was white with fear. One of her girls clung to her nightgown, screaming, but she busily reloaded for Peter.

The Indians were riding past the cabin, taunting the gunmen, with their riding tricks to stay out of the line of fire. The men could see the horses, but not the riders, until the arrow or the gunshot came.

When Daniel heard the thud against the back wall of the cabin, he shouted to Otto who was manning the small gunport, "What's going on back there?"

Otto looked, and his blood ran cold. The raiders in back were shooting flaming arrows at the cabin. His mind raced as he tried to decide what to do. Already smoke was beginning to seep through the tiny chinks.

Daniel ordered the older children to get rags and dip them into the water barrel on the other wall of the cabin where the kitchen things were. "Put them over your faces and lay down on the floor!" he shouted over the pandemonium. *What do we do when it gets too hot to stay in here? Think, Daniel, think.* He tried to remember the landscape behind the cabin. How far was it to the creek? To the woods beyond it? Was there any other place of safety? The five adults, Mary Anna's two half-brothers and three half-sisters, and his two small ones. Seven children and five adults. He groaned. The smoke was getting thicker, and he was beginning to cough, too.

Sudden silence from the raiders and their retreat gave a surge of hope to Daniel. Were they going? Or was it a trick? Wait until they were forced out and then hit them again? He peered through the gunport hole. "What's going on in front?" he asked Peter.

"They're pulling back. Is it a trick?" He looked at Daniel for information about Indian fighting.

Daniel looked at Otto. "Is it?"

"Yup. They're jest awaiting fer it to git too hot in here." His face was grim.

Daniel ran to the back and felt the heat coming off the logs and the sinister cracking of the roof. "Makes no difference, we're going to have to get out of here."

"We can't go out the front, that's for sure." Peter squinted one eye and peered out again to confirm what Otto had said. "Time to start doing some serious praying."

The wind made the war feathers in the braves' hair dance gracefully. The Comanche were covered in colorful paint, each man with a different design. Even the horses were decorated with paint and fluttering strips of cloth woven in their manes and tails.

"Fearsome looking, they are," said Peter with awe. "Just sittin' there on those ponies, waiting." The silence was nerve-wracking.

Daniel hurried to his tool chest and took out a one-man saw. When Peter saw what he intended to do, he took over the window gunport. The logs were hot, putting off enough heat to cook a deer, but the two men hacked at the burning logs until the first one fell to the outside. Quickly water was doused around the small opening, and unspoken prayers were sent up to God with the fervor bred from fear of a gruesome death. *Please don't let them come around to the back of the cabin and find us!*

Under his breath Daniel whispered to Peter. "Save some bullets. Don't let them get the women and girls. If you can, save one for each member of your family. I will for mine. And one for yourself." Peter nodded mutely. Daniel knew there was no need to remind Otto to save a bullet.

"Stay low and run for the creek. Make for the woods as fast

and as quietly as you can. We've got to get into the woods."
There was an ominous crack overhead as the fire ate through
some of the supporting logs. "Go!"

Through the sooty, still-hot logs, the women and children
crawled and ran for the creek and the haven of the woods,
staying as low as they could.

As Daniel, Otto, and Peter climbed though, the battle shrieks
of the Comanche started again, spurring the men into a dead
run. Shots were ringing out, but no one was coming around to
the back.

Mary Anna's nightgown was soaked up to her waist, and
she was covered in greasy soot. Her lungs ached from the smoke,
but she had Columbus in one arm and the baby clutched in the
other as she sped into the woods. Leaves and small branches
tore at her face and clothes. Thorns like living hands ripped at
her ankles, tripping her and tearing the flesh. She ran for the
hollow where she had seen the young girl giving birth. Louisa
was right behind her with her children. They crashed and
thrashed their way through the undergrowth until they could
run no more.

*Even if I'm about to die, I don't think I can go another step.
Lord, help us!* She fell heavily to the ground, turning so as not
to fall on the boys. A rock bit deeply into her shoulder and the
fall knocked the wind out of her momentarily. She could see
her father, Otto, and Daniel coming in, too.

"Are we all here?" she asked softly. They could still hear
gunfire coming from the front of the cabin. The men were
stretched out on the ground facing the cabin though the brush.

Louisa was silently crying and rocking her youngest child in
her lap. Her hair had come loose from her night braid and flew
wildly around her dirty face. The tears made odd tracks through
the dirt. "We're all here, I think," she said, gulping in air and
letting out tears. "Who is shooting?"

"Praise the Lord!" exclaimed Peter. "It's soldiers! I can see them riding after the Indians! It's soldiers!" he shouted and stood up.

Daniel stepped to the edge of the woods, waiting in their safety as three men rode toward them. The horses' hooves made a clicking noise as they stepped across the rocks in the stream.

"Everyone all right?" called the lieutenant in charge. He rode up close to Daniel and dismounted. "Early morning callers, sir?" he asked grimly.

Mary Anna moved to the edge where she could see her worldly goods being offered up like a morning sacrifice to a pagan god. Her eyes were red and dry as she walked to the lieutenant. "Thank you for coming when you did. The Lord surely sent you to us."

"Yes, ma'am, He did. We don't usually patrol this area this time of the morning, but we had to go into Stephenville, and we saw your smoke and heard the gunfire." Ruefully he looked at the cabin. "Sorry we couldn't have been here a lot sooner."

"Don't be sorry, Lieutenant. You saved our lives. For that we thank you and the Lord."

Falling timbers fell into the shell of the cabin, sending a shower of sparks high in the air. The stench of burned meat and damp logs, of trunks filled with clothes filled the air. Bottles popped from the heat. Pages of a book floated, half burned, over the cabin and landed near the creek. All the small crowd of people could do was watch. They could see the skeleton of the Garland's wagon in front of the cabin. The iron wheels were turned inward and leaning on each other as the wood was consumed from them. Over all of this floated a black cloud of smoke. Smoke that spoke of the ruin of their possessions, and the cloud that had saved their lives.

Mary Anna sank to her knees and folded her hands. One by one the rest followed. "Thank You, heavenly Father, for Your care. Thank You for sending these fine men to rescue us, for they are Your army here on earth for the settlers. Angels in blue uniforms. Amen."

The lieutenant put his hat back on and said gallantly, "Thank you, ma'am." Turning to Daniel he asked, "Is there somewhere we can take you? To town, perhaps?"

Daniel looked around at his bedraggled family. There was no place else to go. Fear sparked his eyes. "The Wests! Lieutenant, you've got to send some men to see about the Wests!"

The lieutenant shouted some orders and half his men mounted up to head for the Wests' cabin. "Let's get you to town and get you settled."

The families huddled in the rattling wagon, sitting on and around the supplies for the army post, as it took them to Stephenville. Daniel and Mary Anna watched their smoldering cabin disappear into the distance. They looked at each other, and Mary Anna saw tears in Daniel's eyes. "It's all gone," he whispered as he held her close. "It's all gone."

"What are we going to do?"

"I don't know. I don't know." He shook his head as they went around a bend that shut off the sight of the pile of ashes that had been their home.

Mary Anna was numb. Her only thought was to get to town quickly and stay there. Maybe for a long time. Maybe forever. Maybe their dream was supposed to come true in the town, and not out in the wilderness. A germ of hope seeded itself in her mind.

eleven

When they arrived in Stephenville, the Thorntons and Garlands found clothes for everyone, and town families took them in. Otto made arrangements to stay with another family close to Miss Gilbert's house. He wasn't unhappy about that. Perhaps he would have time to do some serious wooing.

While they all had places to stay, they knew it wouldn't be for long. Their presence crowded the host families, and even frontier courtesy had its limits.

Neither was the horror of the early morning attack easily forgotten. The children had persistent nightmares, and Mary Anna woke, hearing screams in the night.

Daniel, Otto, and Peter were sitting around the pot-bellied stove in the general store with some of the other men. They all knew the story of the raid.

"Thinking of staying in town?" asked Bill, the owner.

"I am," answered Peter. "I'm thinkin' of opening a hotel."

His enthusiasm began to grow as the men around the stove nodded their heads in agreement.

"I can see it now. Finer than the one we sold in Tennessee Colony. Mary Anna can do the cooking again. Ah, it'll be grand to have us all together like it used to be."

"And what will I do?" Daniel asked, his voice heavy with bitterness.

"How about setting up a livery stable and raising cattle for our meat and milk at the hotel?" Peter said reasonably.

"We could use a good hotel," Bill said.

One man standing in back of the larger group made an ugly sound with his mouth. "Iffen it wuz me, I'd be out huntin' me down some red meat, not raising it." He spit an admirable spurt of tobacco into the spittoon from an eyebrow-lifting distance. Some of it dribbled down his dirty beard and he wiped it away with an equally dirty hand.

"Seems to me if them Injuns are gonna burn us out one at a time, we oughter jest go over to that there reservation and help ourselves to a few scalps ourselves. Mebbe it would make 'em think twice before raiding agin." His eyes were serpentine slits, a cold glitter lighting them. His hat hid most of his face, along with his beard, but those eyes burned with hatred.

"You're talking about a government protected place. A peace treaty promises them safety there," Bill objected.

"Yeah, a place where they can hide after they burn and kill and destroy." He turned his stare toward Daniel. "What do you think would have happened to you and your family if them soldiers hadn't come along?"

A shudder passed through Daniel's body. There was no need to answer. All the men knew.

"But why do they kill and then mutilate the bodies so bad?" asked Bill. "And I can't understand torturing any human being."

The man spat another stream of tobacco, but it missed the mark and slid down on the floor. "They kill to make themselves more powerful in the tribe. They mutilate so the dead person cain't be recognized and git into the next land."

"You seem to know a lot about the Comanche," Bill said softly.

The man nodded. "Make it my bidness to know all I can."

Otto noticed the man never seemed to blink, adding to his snake-like appearance. He measured the man with his eyes and found him a person without a soul. Something in his life had robbed him of the last grain of kindness or compassion. It was probably something about the Indians, but no one was going to ask him.

"I like to pay back the Injuns any time I have the opportunity, gentlemen," the stranger added. He took off his greasy hat and the men gasped. The entire top of his head was one large scar. His hair was gone. "I like to take me a scalp ever' now and then to replace the one I lost. I ain't gonna show you the rest of my scars. All you need to know is that I survived. And I'm here to help anyone who wants to do any payin' back." He looked directly at Daniel.

Daniel felt the swirl of emotions he had so carefully guarded become a tornado of anger. Anger at the Indians, anger at the total loss of his home and possessions and the back-breaking labor he had used to begin his kingdom.

"First time I was wiped out, they took all my stock. This time they took everything. Only thing I have is my family, and for that I'm grateful, but how am I going to take care of them now that the Indians have burned me out?" All the frustration, hatred, fear, and anger moved up through him like pus to a boil.

"Why don't we pay them a little call?" the stranger suggested. "Kill us a few women and braves. Take their little ones to make white." He tipped his head and spread his hands wide in a gesture of questioning.

"I don't know," Bill said hesitantly. "We're getting into some deep water here. Doing what they do don't make it right."

"You don't have to go iffen you don't want to," the stranger replied in a condescending tone.

Boots scraping the floor was the only sound in the room for a few seconds, then someone offered hesitantly, "If the army isn't going to be able to help us, maybe we do have to help ourselves."

Daniel let out a long breath and unclenched his fists. The memory of the harrowing raid, the noise, the smell, the fear came crashing through his brain with deadly clarity. He began to tremble and sweat. He could taste the hatred in his mouth for the men who had been a constant threat to his family's existence. But in his mind's eye he could see one man, his face painted with black circles around his eyes and yellow stripes across his forehead, pulling on his bow, an arrow aflame with fire, aiming for Daniel's cabin. That man had wanted to burn Daniel and his family to death. He'd wanted to kill them all. Through clenched teeth Daniel asked, "Peter?"

Daniel's overpowering anger spread from one man to another, and Peter's encounter with the Indians had been so recent that he exploded with his anger. "I'll organize it and lead it. No one is going to burn out my daughter and her family!"

News went from one man to another all over town. The sheriff's pleas went unheard in the tide of fury that swept the town. The men, loaded with ammunition and every weapon they could find, pounded out of town like an avenging army to kill the men who had killed so many of them. The dust around them was like a cloud of energy, charging each man to the depths of fury needed to murder.

Peter planned the raid well. They waited until dawn at the edge of the reservation on the Brazos, whipping themselves into a frenzy. But when they swept down on the camp, it wasn't the raiding warriors who were killed. Men who had never killed anything but a deer or a buffalo murdered two young warriors, eight women and two children, one old man, and several horses. Peter led them on their glorious raid, but later no one would tell of the things that happened. No one wanted to remember that he had been part of such a holocaust on the innocent.

The men were gone and back so quickly, each one wondered if he had experienced a nightmare of epic proportions. Only the stranger had howled with joy as he had slaughtered the tribe. But when the men had ridden back into town, the stranger had not been with them. He had disappeared as he had appeared. And after it was over, no one could explain why men of stature and honor had done such a dishonorable deed.

Daniel was riding away from the massacre, running away from the ghastly scene. He saw three braves riding toward him on their way back to camp. He veered from them, heading into some brush. *Where are the other men?* he worried. He was alone, and there were three men coming to kill him for killing their people. Terror became his body, the living thing that covered him and gave him the power to run. He saw a plum thicket up ahead. As his horse passed it, he jumped off and into its thick bracket, hoping the men would follow his horse. It only put them off for a minute. Then they returned, calling to him, "John, come out, John. We won't hurt you."

Daniel was so terrorized every sense was heightened. He had almost stopped breathing in his efforts to stay hidden.

Then the arrows flew into the thicket. The first ones missed, but one arrow found its mark, slicing Daniel's forearm to the bone. Pain screamed through his body. In a way he was almost glad he had been hit. The pain had a cauterizing effect on his conscience. When the men finally went away to help their people, he whistled for his horse and passed out saying, "Mary Anna. Forgive me, Mary Anna."

His horse took him to the house where they were staying.

"Daniel! Where have you and Papa been? What happened? Oh, dear Lord, you look terrible. What happened? Talk to me!" Mary Anna came out and got him into the house.

When he finally regained consciousness, his eyes were hollow with horror and his head rang with the sounds of death. Of babies screaming. He couldn't get the sound of the babies out of his head.

Neither could he look Mary Anna in the eye. He kept his eyes averted, but when his gaze came to rest on his baby son, the pain exploded into tears. "Oh, what have I done, what have I done?" Tears of bitterness scalded his face with shame.

Mary Anna was shocked, but she continued to tend his wounds and comfort him as though it were the most normal thing in the world for her husband to cry with a broken heart.

A soft knock sounded on the door, and Frances came in. Her silvery hair shone in the lamplight and her kind face was filled with pity. "Do you know what happened?"

"No." Mary Anna wanted desperately not to believe what she thought.

Frances sat down carefully in the rocking chair and in a sad voice told the story of the raid. "I saw them riding out of here, tall in the saddle, like knights in shining armor. And I saw them come back in. Slumped and broken like. They were not proud of what they had done."

Frances was a widow and spent her time in acts of kindness for others. She rose and took Mary Anna in her arms to comfort her. "Don't be hard on him. He'll punish himself much harder than you ever could. He needs your love right now. And your understanding. Even if you don't understand."

There were tears of compassion in her eyes as she patted Mary Anna's hand and left.

The next day Daniel was still in and out of consciousness, but Peter came to call. He was blustery about the raid.

"It had to be done, daughter," he declared confidently, but he couldn't look her in the face, either. His face was flaming with shame. Less certainly he pleaded, "You have to understand how it was there at the store. What the man said was right. If they raid us, then we should raid them. Then they will leave us alone."

Mary Anna's cheeks were red with anger, and she had to hold the knob of the bedstead to stop her trembling. Her voice was low and cold. "When does it stop, Papa, this killing? Where will the circle stop? We are not speaking of animals. We are speaking of people. God's people. No, they're not like us. How could they be? I heard there were women and babies and old people out there. You killed babies? Papa, how could you? How could Daniel? How could anyone?"

She shuddered. "It doesn't matter what they did to us. The circle must be broken. If it isn't, then it means we will all have to die. All of us. And then who will own the land? Who will build your precious hotel or ranch?" She had not yet vented all her fury. It felt like a volcano in her chest, and she was afraid it would literally blow her apart if she let it go.

Peter watched the hatred in his daughter's eyes grow. Her blue eyes blazed with an intensity he had never seen. He knew she would never love and respect him as she once had. And he knew he deserved all of her hatred. He hated himself. Louisa hated him. He put out his hand to reach for her, to try to explain, but Mary Anna turned her back.

Tears flowed down his cheeks as he left silently.

Mary Anna knew it was wrong to turn her back on her father, but she couldn't stand the sight of this man she suddenly didn't know. She looked down at Daniel. Would she be able to love him? How could she ever respect him again? How could she ever stand for him to touch her again?

She moved closer to his bed and looked hard at his face. It was twisted with torment as he dreamed the ugliness of his life over again. She thought of the first time they met. When he first held her in his arms. Their happiness in their first cabin with the baby. She held on to the vision of the man she knew and loved, trying not to see this one in front of her. Her eyes filled with tears. It was the first time she had ever given in and cried with grief. And she reached for the only One who could help her.

Lord Jesus, Who loves us all, help me to love this man. He's my husband and the father of my children. I don't understand what he's done. Maybe You do. I don't want to understand, I just want to be able to forgive him and help him to forgive himself. Give him the love and faith he needs to be able to live with himself again.

Peace flowed through her. Slowly she picked up Daniel's

limp hand, hoping some of the peace she felt would flow through her into his heart.

She remembered telling Virginia how she felt she was sinking in the water like Peter. How long ago that seemed! She closed her eyes and reached out for the Lord as Peter had on that lake so long ago. She could feel His goodness and mercy surrounding her, and trust replaced the doubts she'd had. She belonged out here in the wilderness with Daniel. The Lord would take care of them. He wouldn't shield them from dangerous events, but He would use those trials to build their trust in Him. His hand was there, pulling them both out of the icy water.

Daniel stirred in his sleep, restless in his pain. She took some of the willow tea and spooned a little into his mouth, urging him to swallow it. Then she checked his bandage and washed his face gently. She looked at his face, really looked at it. It was still the face she had fallen in love with in Tennessee Colony. It was the face of her husband. The father of her children. And she loved him. Her heart ached for him, for she had seen the beginning of his pain.

Daniel opened his eyes at her touch. "Mary Anna," was all he could say before the tears began.

"Shh, shh. I know, my darling, I know. It's going to be all right." She softly wiped away his tears. "Some people return to the Lord easily. Some have to do it the hard way. You chose a hard way, my sweet husband, but God has never let go of you. I guess He had to use the big artillery to get your attention. He loves you, Daniel, and forgives you. And so do I."

With his good hand, Daniel lifted her fingers to his mouth and kissed them one at a time with his eyes closed in concentration on the loving task. "I'm sure the Lord does love me. He gave me you."

"We have a lot of things to discuss, my love." She smoothed back a straying lock of hair from his forehead. "And the Lord has given us this time, while you're recuperating." Gently she kissed his forehead where her hand had caressed his hair. "We're going to start over. Everything."

He gave her a weak smile. "Everything?"

"Well, not everything," she conceded. "But our lives. Daniel, let's not rebuild in the same place. There's no reason to live on the Indian's highway. Can't we go somewhere else?"

"Heard the men speaking of the North Bosque. Pretty up there. Not so many Indians." He looked up into her eyes, matching her hope with his pain. "I know them as people now. I saw too much of their humanity. I never saw them as people before. They were a nuisance, like rats or something. Then I saw them as families. Like ours. And their blood."

He closed his eyes in horror. "Dear Lord, their blood, everywhere." He took a steadying breath. "I don't want to fight with them. I just want a place where I can build my ranch and bring up my family. Let's go to the North Bosque. We can start over. I can start over." He smiled tiredly. "You were right about the Lord using the big artillery on me."

"But He didn't sink your boat, Daniel. He pulled both of us back into it with Him. We're back in His boat again. We're together with Him."

With as much vigor as he could muster, Daniel said, "Look out, world. Here comes the Thornton boat with the Lord doing the rowing!"

"Yes, that's the right way to begin. You sleep now, and I'll sit here with you."

"No, come lie beside me," he said softly. His eyes were glazed with pain, but he said, "I still can't believe you're mine."

Deep pain that had nothing to do with his wound came into his eyes. "I'll make it up to you somehow, Mary Anna. I know I did a terrible thing. An unforgivable thing."

She gently laid her finger on his lips. "There is only one thing God can't forgive: not acknowledging him as Lord and

Savior. He has already forgiven you." She took a deep breath. "And I have forgiven you, too. It may be a long time until I forget. Maybe I won't ever forget. But I do love you and I see your sorrow, too."

She nestled against him. "I think the one who will be the last to forgive you is yourself. But if you let the Lord work in you, healing will come." She rested her arm across his chest and her head in the crook of his neck. She could feel his warm tears and she hugged him tightly.

His voice was soft and whispery. "Lord, I do believe You love me and forgive me. I'm more sorry than I can say for what I did. Help me to change my life and my ideas about the Indians. I'm afraid it will be a powerful task, but Mary Anna says You will do it. And God, thank You for Mary Anna."

He had to stop for a moment because the tears were making a huge lump in his throat. "She is more than I could ever deserve." Then he broke down and cried hard, pressing his face into Mary Anna's shoulder.

She couldn't say a thing, but cried silently with him. All her waiting was being rewarded. Daniel was returning to the Lord and asking His forgiveness. Peace flowed through her and around her, and for one wonderful moment, she thought she might die of happiness. Life was going to be too beautiful for words. The Lord had used an awful, bloody event to completely remake Daniel. It had been a high price to pay for serenity. And then she remembered the price Jesus had paid for the sins of the entire world. And she wept in gratitude.

twelve

The next day Mary Anna and Daniel were still walking in a glow of renewal when she had a terrible thought. She was changing his dressing when she voiced her concern.

"Daniel, do you think there'll be trouble about this? You did raid a reservation. Will the army take any action?"

"I doubt it. They're probably glad to have someone to help them settle the Indians down."

"And what about the sheriff? I heard he tried to stop you."

"Yes, but why would he care?"

"I don't know, I just have a funny feeling about all this. Reservations are government land, and there's laws protecting them. It's already all over the county about the raid."

His pale face blanched. "And what are people saying?"

She turned away from him so he couldn't see her face. "Oh, different things," she hedged.

"Like what?"

"Some are for it, and some are against it. You can't go by what you hear."

"Turn around and look at me," he ordered. The worry on her face told him what he needed to know.

"There's talk of retaliation by the Indians?"

"No. There is a rumor that Judge Battles in Waco has issued warrants for the arrest of Papa and you and all the men who were in the raid."

Daniel's face was somber. He wrestled with his new view of the Indians against what he had felt right after the raid on his cabin. "What we did was wrong, but it is fair in the face of what the Indians have done to all of us. We're supposed to be

126

protected by the army from harm from the Indians, too. I don't see any arrest warrants being issued by any judges for them."

"Daniel, what if they do execute those warrants? You could go to trial for this. And if they find you guilty. . ."

"Call your father in here for me. We need to talk."

In a short while Peter was at Daniel's bedside.

"Well, what do you think?" Daniel asked his father-in-law.

Peter took a deep breath, avoiding Daniel's eyes. "I think we could be in big trouble if this judge carries on with this."

"What can we do?"

"Let's talk around the town, explain our side to the people. Since the massacre of the Jackson family outside town, people might not be so quick to judge us harshly." He walked over to the window and stared out unseeingly.

"There isn't a single family out here that hasn't had some horrible thing done to them by the Indians." He turned back to face Daniel, his eyes flinty blue and cold as he said, "I don't intend to go to jail for doing the same thing the Indians are doing."

"But we're supposed to be the law-abiding ones," Daniel argued. He was propped up on pillows, pale and weak and worried. "If we go to jail, what will happen to our families?"

"If we go to jail for protecting our families, no one out here is safe. We might as well all go back to Tennessee Colony," Peter stated flatly.

Daniel wrinkled his brow. The pain in his arm made his mind work more slowly. "Will the sheriff execute the warrant?"

"No. He's on our side."

"Then who would do it?"

"Mr. Neighbors, the Indian agent, has been writing to Governor Runnels. They're trying to get Captain Ford to do it, but he says it's a civil affair and he doesn't have any authority." A smile gleamed in the cold eyes, warming them briefly. "Divide and conquer."

There was no smile in Daniel's eyes. "I don't want to go to trial for this. What's done has been done by both sides. It should be over."

Peter sat down in Mary Anna's rocking chair. "I think we can make it plain to everyone that we don't intend to be dragged through two counties to stand before Judge Battles in Waco. I'll talk to the others." He rose and placed his right hand on Daniel's good arm. "Now, son, you just rest and let me take care of everything. Rest."

Mary Anna came in right after her father left. "Well?"

"Your father is going to get the other men together and let it be known to all that we won't allow ourselves to be arrested and taken to Waco for trial."

"And what will you do if the army comes in here to arrest you? Shoot them, too?"

Daniel grimaced. "Of course not. All we did was protect what was ours."

"You killed women and children on a protected reservation."

He looked at her with pain in his eyes. "At the time it seemed to be the right thing to do. The Indians were raiding us in our homes, so we raided them in theirs. They've killed our women and children, and we killed theirs."

He shuddered. "It sounded so simple and just. I never dreamed it would turn out like this." He lay back in the pillows and covered his face with the hand of his good arm. A groan escaped through the closed fingers. "We can't take on the army. And if they take us to Waco, where they're not having problems with the Indians, they're liable to find us guilty and then jail us or hang us."

"Oh, Daniel, don't talk like that!" Mary Anna fell on her knees beside his bed and buried her face in the covers. "You'd get a fair trial. People can read the newspapers. They know what's going on out here in the west."

"I hope you're right." He looked in her face with new hope.

"The Lord will take care of it. He's the only one who can. Right?"

"Absolutely." She bent to kiss him. "You are learning quickly, my love."

A few days later, Peter was back with more news. There was a bit of a predatory gleam in his eyes. "I think we've created a tempest in the teapot of politics."

"Oh? Is this good news?"

"It seems Captain Ford has refused to come in and arrest us."

"He told the governor this?"

"In a polite and diplomatic way. He said he thought they should try other things first. The sheriff won't do it, Captain Ford won't do it, and now they're trying to get Major Thomas to come help. Only he can't, because he's short of men."

"Let's end this thing, Peter. Let's publish a letter stating our side of it."

"I don't intend to leave Palo Pinto County."

"Let's put that in there. Reach some sort of compromise."

Peter frowned. "It's near to time for the men to be working their farms. No one wants to leave now. Can't. Mary Anna," he called.

"Yes?"

"Get us some paper and a quill and ink. We're going to try to get this thing settled." He looked sternly at Daniel. "I intend to be the one to put my name on this. I feel responsible for the whole thing, in a way. I'm an army man. I was in charge of the raid. Planned it. And I'll be the one to stand up and take the blame, if there's blame to be taken."

Daniel closed his eyes and sighed deeply. "All right. But I'll be by your side all the way. I was there that day, too."

They made a rough draft of a letter to be sent to Governor Runnels. It was circulated among the other men involved and each one had some say about it. New ideas were incorporated and new arguments made until it said all the things they thought were important.

"We need to let the governor know that the army can't always protect us. It takes a civilian group to help," Peter said to the assembled men. "I suggest we call ourselves the Frontier Gards."

"That will give us more dignity than a raggedy band of raiders," agreed one of the men. "I'm fer it."

And so a strong letter defending their actions and agreeing to go to trial, but only in Stephenville, Palo Pinto, or the Jamison Peak, was sent.

It included a protest about Major Neighbors not allowing an Indian on the reservation to be arrested for the murder of Allen Johnson's son and stated firmly that the citizens of Palo Pinto County and the surrounding counties concurred with them fully in their views of their right to defend themselves however they had to. It was signed, "Peter Garland Company, The Frontier Gards."

It took a long time for the letter to get to Governor Runnels, and longer for any type of response.

In the meantime, the men let it be known far and wide that they had no intention of giving up peacefully to the army or any other authority. If they were to go to trial, it would be on their own terms and in their own territory, where they were fairly certain they would be found guiltless.

Mary Anna prayed incessantly for strength to endure and that the men would be found innocent if they went to trial.

Please, God, I know they did something terrible. I also know that Daniel is sorry for his part in it. Maybe even Father. But now they have their backs to the wall. It's true the Indian Agent won't let that Indian be arrested for the murder of a white man. It wouldn't be fair to make them go to trial for killing the Indians.

Help us, Lord. Please. I couldn't live without Daniel. Not even one day. I know he'll never do anything like that again. He's sorry, Lord, and You know that. Please, Please don't take Daniel from me. Let us live out our lives together until we're old and gray and sitting on the porch in matching rocking chairs.

She wiped the tears from her eyes and prayed pieces of the same prayer over and over as she worked and took care of the family. She reminded God that they were planning to move as soon as Daniel was able. To get away from the Indian problems. To get away from the killing. She felt time slipping away, for she knew she would have another child soon. She wanted everything settled before the baby was born. Then they could pick up and go on.

Time dragged. The sheriff wasn't any help when it came to information.

"I don't know a thing," he said honestly when Peter asked him about the warrant being served. "It's in the army's hands now."

Daniel turned to leave, but the sheriff continued. "Of course, you've heard about the army, I guess."

"No, what?"

"There's a lot of hoop-de-la in the South about the government trying to abolish slavery. Lots of unrest. So much, in fact, that the government is beginning to pull a few of the troops out of Texas to help with the problems in the South. The South is threatening to secede from the Union if the North doesn't leave them alone."

"Some of the troops are leaving?"

"Kind of good news and bad news, eh? Gets the army off your back, but puts all of us in danger of more Indian raids."

Daniel walked slowly out of the sheriff's office with new resolve. *Even if I'm not up to par, we've got to get out of here while we still can. I've got to get my family to the North Bosque. If Peter goes with us, we can get the cabins up quicker, and maybe the army will forget all about us.* He hurried as quickly as he could to tell Mary Anna about his plans.

They held a full family meeting with all the adults. Daniel made his proposal, and there was only a small hesitation in Peter's agreement to it.

"Pulling out of here means leaving all these people less protection. It's safer with more of us out here. We'll be letting them down."

"Maybe some of them will go with us. Maybe they'll see things the way we do."

Peter folded his arms in front of his chest and his spreading, middle-aged belly. "Are you running?"

"Yes, but not from the law. I believe the army would call it a strategic relocation. We've got to get off the Indians' highway to Mexico." Daniel's face held firm resolve and certainty. "I don't want to die out here. I came west to build a ranch, and so far I haven't accomplished anything I've set out to do. Maybe the Lord is trying to tell me something."

"The Lord? And when did you get on such familiar terms with the Lord," Peter asked sarcastically.

"Since He let me live through the raid and see how wrong I was about the Indians."

"Wrong!" Peter's face turned almost purple with anger. "How dare you say we were wrong to avenge our dead!"

"It was wrong for me. Seeing those dead women and babies made me see things in a whole different light, Peter." He looked hard at his father-in-law. "Surely it's changed you, too."

Peter dropped his murderous stare. "No. I still think we did the right thing." His chest heaved with his deep sigh. "Well, maybe it wasn't the right thing to do, but it was a necessary thing to do."

He looked Daniel in the eyes. "I'm sorry it turned out like it did. But I thought at the time it was the right thing to do. I can't take back what I did. But each day I pray that Mary Anna can forgive me. I've let her down terribly. I think she still loves me, but it will be a long time of healing before things are the same between us again. Maybe never," he added sadly.

"But I do see the good reasoning behind leaving this area now that the army is beginning to pull back," Peter added. "Things'll only get worse. I agree with you. I didn't come out here to be an Indian fighter. I wanted to build a fine hotel." He almost grinned. "And I doubt the Indians have the money to stay in one of my fine rooms." He looked at Daniel hopefully. "You're sure it's all right with Mary Anna if we go with you to the new place?"

"I'm sure. We've already talked about it. She's a loving woman. Just give her a little time. And she does love you. Okay?" He clapped Peter on the back.

Peter nodded his head and said, "You're a fine man, too, Daniel Thornton."

"All right," Daniel replied in a somewhat embarrassed voice, "no sense in wasting time. Let's get to bed and pack things up in the morning."

"Guess if the army wants us, they'll know where to find us," Peter said philosophically. "But I don't think they're going to have time to fool with us now."

Daniel told Mary Anna about Peter and Louisa wanting to go with them.

Mary Anna gave Daniel a weak smile. "Maybe this is God's way of settling things." Her smile strengthened. "We can make a brand new start. We're smarter now. We've been through 'most everything." She laughed. "The Lord is giving us a chance to build that kingdom you spoke of so long ago on that blanket at the dinner on the ground." And in her heart she thanked God that she and Daniel would be allowed to grow old in those rockers after all.

≈

The next morning at sunrise the adults began packing the few basic things the townspeople had gathered up for them. Daniel had bartered his gold watch for a wagon and two mules to pull it.

"I'll keep the watch for you, Daniel, until you can come back with the cash to get it." Jeb looked steadily at Daniel. "I know how much this watch must mean to you."

Daniel nodded gratefully. "Yes, it was my father's. Thanks for the help, Jeb."

The little boys had no idea what was happening, but the festive air made them happy, too.

About midday, Caleb came by the boardinghouse.

He stepped up on the porch and took off his hat to Mary Anna.

"Morning, Caleb," she smiled.

"Heard you wuz fixing to move up on the North Bosque. Thought I'd come by to say fare thee well." His face revealed the sadness in his heart. "Can't hardly stand for you to leave. Virginia said to tell you good-bye. Her heart is about broke."

"I'm sorry you feel so bad about us leaving," Daniel replied. "It won't be the same without you and your fine family. You know, Mary Anna and I were talking about this just the other night. How it isn't going to be safe out here with so many leaving. We were wondering if maybe you and Virginia might care to come along with us and build close by. We've a mind to put up a sort of little town of our own with her family. We'd be so happy, and so much safer, if you'd come along."

Caleb's face lit up like a boy with a new puppy. "Well, now that you mention it, Virginia and I did talk some about moving away from this place, too. We hadn't made up our minds yet about which direction to go. Might as well go with good friends, I always say. It's way past friendly for you to invite us, and we'd be more than pleased to go with you to the new promised land. I'll just hurry and go tell Virginia. We don't have much. We can be ready to travel whenever you are."

His eyes shone and his smile went clear across his face from one big ear to the other. "Whoooooeeee!" he shouted. "We got us a wagon train!" And he jumped off the porch, hit the ground running, and forgot his horse waiting patiently at the rail.

Mary Anna hugged Daniel. "I think you made him happy. And I know you made me happy." She kissed his mouth softly. "Thank you, Daniel."

Daniel grinned a little self-consciously. "It just makes good sense. And they're good people. But I'll take the kiss anyhow."

"Speaking of kisses, have you talked with Otto lately?"

Daniel looked at the big smile on her face. "Go on, tell me, I know you're dying to."

"He and Angel are getting married. They've already chosen a little house at the edge of town."

"When?"

"Autumn. Can we come back for the wedding?"

"Why, we couldn't miss that wedding. We've watched this romance blossom from the beginning." Daniel sighed deeply. "Too bad. He was the best hand I ever had." But he grinned when Mary Anna glared at him.

⁊

By the next week, the little caravan of three wagons and assorted animals was ready to make its way along the Brazos to a new promised land.

Daniel was in the saddle of his favorite horse riding beside Mary Anna as she drove their wagon.

"This is the right thing to do, Daniel. I'm certain of it. I prayed that you and I would be able to grow old together in our rocking chairs on the front porch, and this is God's way of making that come true. I couldn't bear to be separated from you even for a day." A chill passed over her. "When I thought of you having to go to jail or, or worse, I couldn't take it. Now I'm sure this is the answer to my prayers."

He grinned broadly at her as he rocked in the saddle. "There's no way you can get rid of me. We promised each other forever, and that's what I'm promising to give you. Besides, I still owe you that star."

"You did promise me a star when we were coming out here," she remembered, smiling. "And I intend to collect it."

"No more than I intend to give it."

thirteen

The three families selected a good spot out in the open, but close to water. The foundation for the first cabin was laid in dog-trot style. There were two rooms connected by a large porch. It was called a dog trot because on a hot day, the dogs could usually be found resting on the cool porch. One room was used for living and cooking, and the other was for sleeping and storage.

"Oh, Daniel!" Mary Anna exclaimed. "I have all the room in the world! It's so big!" She danced around the nearly finished cabin, furnishing and arranging things in her mind.

"And for safety, I used a tin roof. No more fires from arrows," Daniel said soberly. "I've saved a piece of tin to put on the wooden floor under the fancy cooking stove I intend to buy you a little later on. Then we can use the fireplace for warmth, and you can cook like a real lady."

She walked up to him and wrapped her arms around his neck. "Thank you, my darling husband." His blush was seen only by his two boys, and they giggled as they watched their parents embrace.

Caleb assumed Peter's cabin would go up next. There was a stunned silence at Peter's reply.

"Daughter," he looked fondly at Mary Anna, "I think I've brought enough sadness into your life. Louisa is ready to live in the city again. And if I'm to have that hotel, that's where we'll be needing to go. We'll stay here until we get the Wests' cabin up, and then we'll be heading for Young County."

"I know you only came out here to help us get a new start, Papa. I'm grateful for that." Tears gathered in Mary Anna's eyes. "And I also want you to know I'm sorry to see you and Louisa go. I still love you very much, and I have forgiven you. But I know you will be happier in town. We won't be that far apart. We'll see each other now and again."

Through their Herculean labor, the second cabin was ready quickly. It was far enough away for privacy, but close enough for safety. The women planted a communal herb and vegetable garden. Mary Anna and Virginia would dry and make medicine from the herbs.

Then it was time to say good-bye to the Garlands. Louisa held Mary Anna close and said, "I'm sorry I won't be here to see that new little one born. Write me and tell me everything." Love shone in her eyes.

"Virginia will be here with me. I'll be fine. I'll let you know right away if you have a grandson or a granddaughter."

"It'll be a daughter this time. I'm sure," Louisa said.

Hugs and more hugs were exchanged, and then the wagon disappeared down the indentations of grass that served as a road.

❧

The cabins were sitting in a low place close to the river, and the night fog drifted up to the house, bringing with it mosquitoes and mysterious fevers.

September came, but it brought with it more rain to add to the heat. And with the rain came even more mosquitoes. The nights were so sultry it was hard to breathe, but if the door were left open, there was little sleeping because of the drone of the heavy insects.

During the night Mary Anna heard the baby coughing. Daniel woke as she climbed out of bed.

"What is it?"

"Peter is coughing. Will you get me some of that cherry bark syrup I made?"

She sat down in the rocker with little Peter, and Daniel helped her spoon a little of the cough syrup down the baby's throat. "He doesn't feel hot. Maybe he's just teething." She rocked him until he feel asleep again and crawled back in bed with Daniel.

"Are you all right?" His voice was carefully controlled to hide the anxiety he felt. "You've lost weight. Why, by now I should be able to easily see that baby of ours." He didn't mention the dark circles under her eyes or the mild cough she seemed to be developing.

"I'm worn out from the heat and the mosquitoes," she snapped.

Daniel knew when to be quiet, but he slept lightly in case the baby woke so he could be the one to get up with him.

Everyone was short-tempered from lack of sleep and from the constant itching of the large welts the mosquitoes made. Mary Anna concocted a salve from lard and boiled willow root, and it helped some.

She woke one morning, shivering. *The cool weather has finally come,* was her first thought. She got up to check the boys. They were warm enough, but she was thoroughly chilled. When the room began to spin, she realized the temperature of the house had not changed. She had come down with a fever. She crept back to bed and woke Daniel.

"I'll get Virginia," he said as he pulled on his boots.

"Take the boys with you. I don't want them here." It was all she could manage between her chattering teeth.

The world became a hazy place of hot and cold. And then the hot and cold was replaced by hot, ripping pains, ravaging her body. There had been no faint cries, so it couldn't have been the baby. *Besides, it's not time.*

Daniel kept trying to tell her something about everything being all right. She wanted to tell him she was getting better. The terrible pain had stopped and now all she felt was the heat.

But she was so tired. Too tired even to push away the spoon of warm liquid Virginia kept trying to push between her tightly clenched teeth. She wanted to drift with the lovely tide that ebbed and flowed through her. She was too tired to feel guilty that she wasn't taking care of anything for Daniel. If only the heat would go away. It kept pulling at her, sucking away her strength. Daniel kept telling her he needed her, but she couldn't figure out what it was he wanted her to do.

She wanted to invite him to come with her to her nothing-ness land. It would be so lovely with just the two of them. *No, there are the boys. Where are the boys? Virginia must have them. They're fine. Isn't that what Daniel said?*

She drifted on, sorry that Daniel couldn't go with her.

The dream began to fade and she opened her eyes to find Daniel asleep in a chair beside her bed. Why wasn't he in bed with her? She tried to call him, but the effort was too much. His hand on the coverlet was close to hers. Slowly, she moved her fingers to grasp one of his.

He awoke with a start. "Mary Anna! You're awake!" He buried his head in the covers and wept. She was astonished at his crying. She wanted to tell him she had only slept a long while, but he sat on the edge of the bed and cradled her, all the while chanting, "Thank You, God. Thank You."

With tears running down his cheeks, he kissed her gently on the forehead. "I thought I'd lost you!" He held her tenderly and she wanted to ask him many things, but she felt so exhausted. How could she have slept so long and yet be so drained?

Reluctantly he rested her head back on the pillow and hurriedly got a bowl of soup from the big pot in the fireplace. "Here, drink a little of this. You had me scared to death."

Shakily she put her hand up to stop the spoon. "What happened?" she asked in a voice that didn't belong to her.

"You've had a fever. You've been sick for a long time."

"How long?"

"Almost five weeks now." Cautiously he added, "You don't

remember anything, do you?"

"No." From her reclining position she followed his eyes to the flatness of her middle. "I lost the baby." Her voice was expressionless.

"Yes." His eyes filled with tears again. "It was too soon."

"A girl?"

"Yes."

She could feel the tears inside, but they were too far away to spill over onto her cheeks. "I guess we'll never get our girl, will we?"

"Some day, my darling. Some day," he said softly. "Right now all I can think of is that I have you, and I am so thankful for that."

The days passed between healthful sleep and a cautious returning to the real world. Virginia and Daniel took turns nursing Mary Anna. They brought the boys over for brief visits and then hurried them away.

She spent her waking hours regaining her strength and dealing with the news that her baby was dead. Her grief felt odd. No one spoke of the baby. She had to ask Daniel about the little one's birth and burial. His recital was short. And all she could think of to say at its end was, "Another house, another grave." *Lord, your ways are hard. I only get to keep every other child You give me. Take care of her, Lord. Be sure she gets to know her big brother.*

"What month is this?" Mary Anna asked Daniel one morning.

"Beginning of December, why?"

"I went to sleep in the fall and woke up in the winter."

"Guess you know a little of how a bear feels," he grinned.

They were sitting in front of the fire—she still in her nightgown and with a quilt wrapped about her legs and feet.

Daniel watched her carefully, as if to see if she had been damaged by the fever for life. He was gentle with her.

On a December morning when the wind was still and the

sun warmed the earth in a promise of a faraway spring, Mary Anna dressed warmly and went out to the place where Daniel had buried their daughter.

The grave was very tiny, but it was properly marked with a piece of rose limestone. It had come from the same place where they had gathered rocks for the foundation of the cabin. Daniel had smoothed one side and scratched "Thornton" on it.

Daniel watched his wife from the window of the cabin. His heart ached for her, but he left her alone.

She stayed only a short time, but when she returned to the cabin, a great weight had been lifted from her heart. She felt whole again and ready to pick up her life and go on.

"It's time for the boys to come home," she announced as she took off her heavy winter things.

They were a family again, and Mary Anna felt joy beginning to slip back into her heart like tiny sun rays that refused to be held out by clouds.

As she served their noontime meal, Daniel said, "You're filling out nicely." When she bent to kiss him, he added, "There are little roses blooming in your cheeks, too." His grin was broad and his happiness complete to have her whole again.

Five-year-old Columbus and two-year-old Peter were thrilled to be home again. Mary Anna and Daniel decided to have a simple Christmas celebration, and the boys reveled in the furtive activities and accompanying giggling.

Peter was trying to talk. His vocabulary was fairly well developed but didn't always come out the way he wanted it to. For no understandable reason, he called his older brother Tump, and no amount of correction could change him. Soon, everyone called Columbus Tump.

Tump adapted quickly to his name change. Mary Anna began teaching him his letters that winter. He learned to spell his new name and then asked to spell Peter's. Mary Anna explained Peter's full name was Thomas Peter, but that they had called him Peter.

"So, the first letter of his name is T and the first letter of his next name is P?" And in the fairness of life, Tump renamed Peter T.P.

"I don't know why I bothered to name those boys at all," Mary Anna grumped to Daniel.

"Why don't you just let them name the next one to start with?" he grinned.

Mary Anna didn't answer. She wasn't sure her heart could stand the risk of another loss.

There was talk now and again of an occasional Indian raid, but none occurred on the North Bosque. Yet the men remained careful when they were out. No one went anywhere without at least a side arm.

The men hunted frequently and kept the smokehouse full of meat and poultry. When Daniel returned from one of those hunts, Caleb met him. Caleb grimly related the story of a raid on a nearby neighbor.

"We're getting together to track those thieves down. They got close to twenty-five horses."

Daniel agreed the raiders should be pursued. The horrors of the retaliation on the reservation were still very much on his mind, and he made it clear that his only goal was to retrieve the horses.

The eight men, Caleb, and Daniel left immediately and tracked for the rest of the day. They made camp and rose at dawn.

At about noon, Daniel said to Caleb, "They seem to be taking the horses to Mexico." There was absolutely no humor in his voice.

"Let's make a noon camp and decide what to do," suggested Henry.

"I had no idea they'd bring them this far," complained O'Brian. "I can't be away from my farm. My family is without any protection."

The other men shook their heads in agreement.

But when night came, they were still a long way from home and the temperature was dropping, with a steady wind picking up.

"Hey, ain't there a schoolhouse that's being built out here somewhere?" Pee Wee asked. "I'm beginning to freeze to death in this here saddle. We could make us a camp there and get out of this cold."

The partially constructed building was found. Knowing there could still be Indians around, the men hid their mounts and saddles and slipped quietly into the building carrying their saddle blankets.

The windows had not been set in the building, nor had the ceiling been closed. Boards were placed loosely on the rafters. The men decided to sleep on the loose boards rather than the cold floor. They'd barely settled down to sleep when Daniel heard a shuffling noise down below. With his heart in his throat, he nudged the man next to him and motioned below.

A large band of Indians, including women and children, were entering the building. Weary and cold, they began preparing for sleep almost immediately, rolling out buffalo robes and blankets.

Frantically the word was passed in the rafters of the settlers' danger. They were outnumbered. There was nothing to do but wait until the Indians slept and then try to slip out of the building.

Cold perspiration ran down Daniel's back as he hugged the board on which he lay. Silently, he prayed that none of the men would accidentally make a noise that would give them away. It seemed an eternity before the tired band of Indians at last fell asleep.

The moonlight glinted now and again on the cold steel of a rifle barrel sticking out of one of the blankets, so Daniel had to assume that each man below was armed. Even if the men had only bows and arrows, Daniel was not eager to feel the bite of an arrowhead again. He concentrated on staying still and breathing as quietly as he could.

Finally the only sound was the soft snoring of deep sleep below. Using hand signals, the settlers agreed to go one at a time down the outside ladder. Daniel would be next to last, and Pee Wee would be last. There was very little breathing as the men slipped out one at a time down the ladder.

When Daniel's turn came, he willed himself to keep his boots totally silent as he eased himself down. His head was level with the boards when he saw Pee Wee start to move toward the exit.

Suddenly Pee Wee's foot slipped, and he fell with the board to the middle of the sleeping band. He leaped through the door frame and began giving orders like he was commanding troops, all the while firing his gun outside the building.

The frightened Indians charged through the doors and windows and quickly vacated the building. One of the Indians threw his tomahawk at Pee Wee as he ran out the door. It stuck in the frame just above Pee Wee's head.

As the Indians fled, the settlers stood frozen by the outside wall. When they finally realized the danger was past, each man collapsed to the ground. Nervous laughter broke out.

"That's the craziest thing I ever saw," said O'Brian shakily.

"Pee Wee, you've got the quickest brain I ever saw," Daniel said in awe. "How'd you think of doing that?"

Pee Wee pulled at his scraggly beard. "Ah, I used to be a scout in my younger days. It just come to me."

The men pounded Pee Wee on the back and laughed with relief.

"Craziest thing I ever saw," was repeated frequently on the long, cold ride home that night.

The story made a sensational hit in the settlement and was told from cabin to cabin with great glee. Soon it was being called the Schoolhouse Scramble, and Pee Wee became a local celebrity for his bravery and quick thinking.

fourteen

Daniel was working in his fields when he saw the small cloud of dust coming toward the cabin that indicated a rider was on the way. He stopped and said to Caleb, "Better start moving toward the cabin."

They were there when an old friend rode up wearing a very sober face.

"Hello, Sheriff," said Daniel cordially. "Get down and have something cool to drink. It's been a long time since we've seen you. What are you doing away from Stephenville?"

The sheriff climbed from his roan and led the horse to the trough for a drink before he eased his own thirst.

"This is not a happy call I'm making on you, Daniel," he said as he sat in one of the rawhide-bottomed cane chairs under the tree. He accepted some cold buttermilk from Mary Anna and took a deep drink.

"I didn't think it was."

"I've come to ask you to give yourself up for trial in Stephenville," he said quietly. "I didn't bring a posse. You're a man of honor. Either you'll come with me or you won't. I didn't want a gunfight over it."

"Have you found any of the other men?"

"Some. I told them the same as you. I won't know about all of them until time for the trial. Some had work they had to finish before they could come in."

"You're a brave man to do this by yourself," Daniel said with honesty.

"No point in having another war over it. I'd like to get this cleared up, and I think you would, too." He eyed Daniel for a response.

"No, I can't say that I am eager to get it over with. I thought of it as over with when I moved up here on the North Bosque."

"Unfortunately the government don't think of it quite that way." He shrugged his shoulders and handed Mary Anna the empty glass. "The trial will be in two weeks. You can get you a lawyer, or you can defend yourself. Up to you." He swung up into the saddle again, tipping his hat to Mary Anna. "Thank you for the buttermilk. I always did love buttermilk." He turned his horse to the west and began another slow ride looking for the next man.

Mary Anna stood frozen in place holding the empty glass.

Caleb looked at Daniel. "Do you know what you're gonna do?"

"No point in pretending they don't care anymore. Guess I'll go in."

"He didn't ask about Father," said Mary Anna. "I wonder if he'll be there."

"I imagine he will if they find him." Daniel walked to the wash bowl set in the side of the cabin to splash his face and hands. "Let's have some dinner and then get that field finished," he said to Caleb as though nothing had just ripped his world apart.

❧

That night in bed there were decisions to be made. Mary Anna was chilled to the bone with the bleak prospects that faced them.

"Are you going to get a lawyer?" she asked.

"I don't know a lawyer. I can tell them what happened. I'm not a deceitful man."

"But lawyers know tricks they can pull and things to do to get people out of trouble." There was panic in her voice.

"I don't need tricks." He looked in her cornflower blue eyes and said, "You're the one who taught me to depend on the

Lord. Well, now will be the most important time we've ever called on Him." He tipped her chin up with his fingertips to kiss her lightly. "I'm depending totally on the Lord. And whatever He decides, that's how it will be."

"Ohhh, Daniel," she wailed. "I know you're right, but this will take most of my time to pray about. I know I can't meet this by myself."

"You'll have to pray and work at the same time," he said reasonably.

"I already do that." She sighed. "This is no teasing matter. They could hang you if they find you guilty." Tears filled her eyes.

He pulled her hard against his broad chest and held her close. "The Lord is in charge of this. Let's ask Him for the strength to face whatever we must. This will be our biggest test of faith ever."

&

As it turned out, Daniel would be tried by himself. The other trials were scheduled for later.

True to his word, he did not hire a lawyer. He prepared himself with prayer and trying to remember exactly what had happened.

A strange quiet permeated Stephenville when Daniel and Mary Anna drove into town with Caleb and Virginia. The children had been left with a neighbor.

People on the wooden sidewalks stopped to look. The Thorntons gave a little wave to familiar faces, and some of the people waved back.

"Town don't seem as friendly as it used to be," remarked Caleb.

"Looks like the whole town is holding its breath," said Virginia.

"I saw some smiling faces," argued Mary Anna.

"Wonder what they were smiling about," Daniel added darkly. Frances Gerald was waiting for them on her porch as they rode up. There was genuine joy in her face when she and Mary Anna and Virginia hugged.

"It's so good to see you again. And don't you worry about that silly trial. Everyone around here knows what kind of people you are. They're not going to find you guilty," she said confidently as she led them to their rooms. "I've been talking to everyone around town. Now don't you worry about a thing." Her blue eyes shone under her snowy white pompadour. "Everything is going to be just fine. It's all in the Lord's hands."

Mary Anna looked at her wistfully. "I'm positive it's in the Lord's hands. I wish I could be so sure Daniel would be found innocent."

❧

It was stuffy in the courtroom. Mary Anna had worn her best dress — the one with the long sleeves and too many petticoats. *Vanity gets me again. I should have worn my simple frock. It would have been so much cooler.*

Daniel didn't look comfortable in his long coat and dress pants. "I think you're the handsomest man in the entire world," Mary Anna had told him. But the clothes did give him a measure of confidence. He didn't look like a county rube.

The prosecuting attorney looked mild-mannered, but had a reputation for high intelligence. Daniel was frightened of him, for this man could have him hanged or put in jail.

Mary Anna stood beside him waiting for the trial to begin. "The judge looks so serious," Mary Anna remarked. "I hope he's a fair judge. If he is, then everything will be all right." Hope shone in her bright blue eyes as she looked up into Daniel's face for confirmation.

"Make no mistake about it. This is a serious trial," he said gravely. "I had no choice but to come in and face this thing. It's in the Lord's hands."

"Order in the court!" said the judge loudly and banged his gavel on top of the table that served as his desk.

Twelve men were chosen for the jury, though Daniel's knowledge of this art was limited to sizing a man up by his eyes and his manner. Once again he had to rely on the Lord for help.

The proceedings were informal. Daniel told his side of the story, and the other attorney challenged him at different points. He was allowed to clarify his answers.

When he got to the part in his story where the men were riding into the reservation and the killing began, he broke down.

"I'm sorry. I can still hear the screams of the women and children. See the blood splattering everywhere. I had hated the Indians for so long, and I didn't think of them as human beings. When I saw where they lived and was in the middle of their family life, shooting and killing, it was like I was in the middle of any family. The one picture that will never go away is of the young mother holding a baby in her arms. I can still see the fear on her face, the way she tried to run, and how she fell when she was shot from behind."

He shuddered and squeezed his eyes shut, trying to make the scene go away. "I could hear the baby screaming after she fell on top of the child." He stopped to gain his composure. "I don't know for sure who I shot or who I killed. I'm grateful to God for that. But I was there when I shouldn't have been. I fired into the village as we rode in. Lots of shots. But after I saw the woman and the baby, I rode out with the braves chasing me.

"I helped plan that raid. I was there. I did a lot of shooting. But I learned something that day. I didn't know my enemy the way I thought I did. I was still hating the men who killed my grandfather, and the men who stole my cattle, and the ones who burned my cabin and tried to kill my family. I should have been fighting them—not the women and children. And not on the reservation. At the time there just didn't seem to be any other way."

The courtroom was quiet. Mary Anna listened intently to her husband confess. She had never been more proud of him.

The attorney asked a few questions, but he could see it would do little good to harangue or harass Daniel. It had been a sincere recital. He simply reminded the jury of their responsibilities and what the law said.

Then the waiting began. It was mercifully short. Mary Anna moved to sit beside Daniel at the table as the jury filed in.

The judge looked questioningly at the jury. "Would the foreman please stand up?" When one man stood, he asked, "Have you reached a verdict?"

The man nodded. Harland Lathman, a man in his middle thirties and foreman of the jury, stood with his maimed hat in his hands. It was black and had a bullet hole through its battered crown. He twisted the hat at finding himself the center of attention of the courtroom. His black hair was slicked down to follow the contours of his bumpy skull, and his mustache had run riot across his upper lip. He had worn an almost clean shirt for this special occasion but had forgotten to put on clean pants, and stains covered both pants legs. His boots bore the unmistakable marks of a true cowboy.

He cleared his throat and shifted his weight from one leg to the other.

"Well, Judge, I mean, Your Honor, we've been studying about this and we did some careful thinking. We feel like it's prob'ly true that Daniel Thornton did go on that raid. And we're sure if he went on the raid as mad as he said, then he was sure to have kilt someone. I've been in some wild fights when ya didn't know fer sure who you was shooting at and if you kilt anyone until the whole thing wuz over.

"We know that he knows that he mighten of kilt some women and children." He paused and looked straight at Daniel, and Daniel felt drops of sweat rise up like raindrops on his brow.

"Now we considered where this happened and when it happened. What went before and after." He took another deep breath but was interrupted by the judge.

"We appreciate that you took so much time in deliberating this case, but all of this should have been done behind closed doors, not now. All you have to do Mr. Lathman is give us the verdict." The judge's face was lightly twisted in a smile. Frontier justice was the common fare of his court.

"Thanks fer remindin' me, Judge, I mean, Your Honor. But I think it's important for the people to understand why we called this thing the way we did." The hat went around a little faster in his hands.

The judge sighed. "Very well, continue."

The hat stopped. "Daniel shouldn't have gone out there 'cause it was protected land. But the Indians should have stayed on that land to start with. They shouldn't have kilt any white people. And they shouldn't have tried to kill the Thorntons or burn down their cabin or steal their stock all the time. But there's one of us on the jury that thinks we shouldn't be out here taking the land from the Indians to begin with." All eyes turned to the only Quaker on the panel, and he blushed deeply but held a firm look in his eyes.

"I don't know what the right and wrong of all this pioneering is about, but I do know the Bible says not to kill."

Daniel felt the sweat begin under his arms, staining his shirt under his coat.

"I guess what the jury wants to know, what most folks want to know, is when is it all going to stop? Feuding like this will not get us anywhere."

The judge was beginning to turn a little sour with all this philosophical rhetoric, but he held still.

Mr. Lathman recognized the impatience of the judge. "So the jist of it is that Daniel is guilty of killing those Indians. And he should be punished for it."

Mary Anna felt the gasp go out of her mouth and the life from her body. Daniel's ramrod straight back went limp.

"But," Mr. Lathman went on, "unless you also bring in them renegade Indians to trial and find them guilty, then you shouldn't punish Mr. Thornton by hisself. So we, the jury find Mr. Thornton guilty, but we don't want him punished."

The courtroom erupted into hoops of joy. It was a popular verdict, and by frontier standards, a just one.

"Order, order in the court!" shouted the judge as he banged his gavel on the table. "Order, or I'll throw you *all* into jail."

Gradually the people settled down to excited quiet whispers and then the silence that the judge had ordered.

He sighed deeply, pondered the verdict of the jury, and looked at Daniel's hopeful face. "The jury has spoken, Mr. Thornton, but I have something to add. We are trying to civilize this part of the United States. This brand of justice will not serve to further that cause. Vigilante activities are not helpful, even in the absence of the army. If that type of justice were turned against you, you would more fully understand the dishonor of your deed."

Daniel's head dropped in shame at the truth of the judge's words.

"I am not going to punish you, as the jury asked me. I saw repentance in your testimony. I believe you know what you did was wrong, and I'm fairly sure you have suffered because of it. My only choice if the jury found you guilty was to hang you. However, I don't think that would serve any good cause. You seem to be an upstanding family man and a hard-working citizen. We can't afford to lose men like you on the frontier. I do need to know. Do you intend to kill a man or woman again in anger? Do you understand that taking the law into your own hands will bring nothing but heartache?"

Daniel stood to his full height and straightened his shoulders. "I understand what I did was wrong, Your Honor. I've lived a lifetime since all that happened. I believe that God has forgiven me for what I did. I will still protect what is mine as long as the Indians continue to steal from me. But I will take back only what belongs to me, and I won't do any killing. I think I've already proven that by what we now call the School-house Scramble." Soft laughter rippled through the courtroom. "I want to thank the men on the jury for listening so carefully to the things I said and maybe some of the things I didn't say, but meant to. My family thanks you, also." He sat down, and the room exploded with happy talk and applause.

Mary Anna turned to Daniel and kissed him fully on the lips. Then she burst into torrents of tears, sopping at them with her lace-hemmed handkerchief. Daniel could hear her soft, *Thank You, God,* murmured over and over to herself.

❧

Later that day, as they were riding out of town, Caleb said, "I notice the people seem a little friendlier," and he smiled his slow cowboy grin.

Mary Anna cuddled next to Daniel in the front. "I was so afraid we were going to be parted, one way or the other. My heart is bursting with the joy of knowing we don't ever have to be apart again."

Daniel slipped his arm around her. "We're together again, my love."

❧

Another story joined that of Daniel's exoneration in traveling as fast as a Texas prairie fire. The government was trying to tell a man how to run his life and business by forbidding slavery. The counterpoint was that no one had the right to own another human being.

When Daniel went into town for supplies, he heard the arguments back and forth around the pot-bellied stove of the general store. It spilled out on the street and around the watering troughs.

He listened as he waited for his supply list to be filled at the general store.

"I'm telling you, there's going to be a war over this," spouted one red-faced citizen to another.

"You tell me that deep down in your heart you think it's okay to buy and sell human flesh just like it was a horse," replied his opponent.

A man with his feet propped up close to the stove spoke.

"Slavery's not the problem. It's the Knights of the Golden Circle causing all the trouble."

"Who are they?" asked Daniel as he leaned on the cluttered counter of the store.

"A secret society." The man's bushy beard was streaked with gray, and he stroked it as he puffed a corn cob pipe. "They go around recruiting new members and then go 'visit' people that don't think like they do. Hung two men in Ft. Worth last week that disagreed with them."

A chill passed through Daniel. "What about the law? Don't they do anything?"

"Some of the law may be members," replied the bewhiskered man quietly. "My name's Johann Wilham." He offered his hand to Daniel.

"Daniel Thornton."

"Exactly what do these men want?" asked the storekeeper, Charlie Billinger.

"Well, Charlie, they want all of us to know that there are some people in Texas that are trying to start a slave uprising. I think they have killed a lot of people who argued with them all over the state."

"But there aren't that many slaves in Texas," Daniel pointed out.

"There are getting to be more all the time," said Johann. "The Knights said they found poison on some of the whites, so they took them to the outskirts of town and hung them, too. They are stirring up trouble."

"Ft. Worth ain't that far away from here," said Charlie nervously. "But I ain't heard of no trouble with the slaves."

All the men nodded their heads in agreement.

"All I know is rumors I picked up when I was back that way last week." Johann sucked slowly at his pipe. "I also heard that they're trying to force old Governor Sam to call a special session of the legislature so they can vote on whether to join in with the South. Of course, they want everyone to vote for it. It could be they are making sure the vote goes their way."

"Houston ain't going to be run around by a bunch of hooligans," said Charlie. "He's made it plain he thinks if we leave the Union we'll get into war and," he added ominously, "a war we can't win. I go along with Sam. If we're going to do something, we ought to just go back to being a republic and stay out of all this."

There was silence as each man weighed the words of their beloved leader. Sam Houston had made his position well known all over the state and been quoted in the papers extensively.

"Gentlemen," began Johann, "I am going to take a step out in faith that none of you belong to the Knights and speak from my heart. I left Germany to get out of all the civil wars. You men aren't Southerners any more. We're all Texans. If the South wants to cut its own throat, let it. We have all we can handle here with the Indians and the Mexican bandit, Juan Cortina, running back and forth across the river.

"I am scared to death of this thing. It is going to get us into war for sure. Here it is the first of January, and it looks like Old Sam is going to have to give the Knights that session. When he does, it's going to be a big fight as to who we join. For me, I think we should be a republic again. Too much blood has been spilt to go back on that."

He looked into the eyes of the closest man. "I know because I was there. And I'm not willing to go fight for something that doesn't concern me. I don't got slaves, and I don't plan to have any." He puffed on his pipe and, a practical German to the end, concluded, "I can't afford them."

Daniel saw men nod their heads at different points in his argument. Covertly he watched to see if he could detect anyone who might be a Knight. It didn't seem likely by their expressions.

"I've still got family in the South. Pickens County, Alabama," he offered quietly.

"I guess a lot of us do," sighed Charlie. "But I have a family

out here that needs me. Got to take care of them first," he
added firmly.

"Well, the South's fight seems pretty clear to me," said Daniel.
"The Union doesn't have the right to take away their way of
making a living. They need those slaves to do the work."

Johann nodded his head in agreement. "True, but still it is a
thorny question. You keep slaves, Mr. Thornton?"

"No," said Daniel. "I'm like you. Can't afford them."

"But you feel the South has the right to own them?" Johann
persisted.

Daniel hesitated. "I guess I think the government doesn't
have the right to come in and tell a man what he ought or
ought not to do with his life."

Most of the men nodded their heads in agreement.

"We're an independent lot, we Texans," noted Johann. He
laughed. "That's how we got to be Texans to start with."

On that note of general agreement, Daniel quit the conversation. It was too big a problem to be solved around a pot-
bellied stove in the rough country of Erath County.

"Been very interesting talking to you, Mr. Wilham," he said
cordially as he gathered up his needed provisions.

As he drove the oxen home, the conflict he had heard was
reflected in his eyes. He thought his way through what he knew
about slavery. *It's so natural. Someone has to do the grueling
work. Slaves are the ones chosen to do that. In return, Pa takes
care of them, gives them food and shelter. He is a temperate
man and has never punished a slave unless he really needed
to. Besides, all good businessmen know better than to let an
expensive slave be damaged any more than he'd let his farm
animals be hurt.*

His father seemed to have a genuine affection for some of
his favorites that had been with him all their lives. The house
servants especially were more like part of the family. *Wasn't I
raised by Tildy? Slaves are just like overgrown children. They
need constant supervision. Except for those special ones, and*

they are treated almost like family, never punished bad or ever sold.

Did the North know about that? How could they know about this way of life?

And yet, Daniel couldn't forget the times he'd seen a mother wailing as her young were sold off or the treatment he'd seen other planters impose on their slaves. Whippings and worse. He shuddered as some of those scenes filled his mind.

By the time he'd gotten home, he'd decided that nothing could be done about any of the problems from way out here in Texas. It was probably just the politicians stirring up the people in order to get re-elected to their places of power. It had no bearing on how he made his living. He kept no slaves. Wanted none.

There was a deep satisfaction in pitting himself against nature and carving out his place in the frontier wilderness. He enjoyed feeling his muscles strain to build his kingdom. He said nothing to Mary Anna about the ugly talk he'd heard.

But Mary Anna was aware of the secession talk. It frightened her to think that something so awful was stalking their horizons while they were snug and warm in their new home.

Even the Indian raids were less frequent. Talk was that the Comanches had been rounded up and moved to another reservation up in the Oklahoma Territory. There were still renegades, but they spent most of their time evading soldiers.

Mary Anna grew larger with their next child, praying this time it would be the girl she longed for and that she would be able to keep the child rather than lay it to rest with the others.

She was beginning to get the soil in her garden ready to plant when her time came. Virginia was with her; Daniel paced outside the door of the bedroom.

It was Virginia's bright smile that told him of his new baby daughter. "She's all right? Both of them, I mean," Daniel stammered.

"Yes. Both of them are fine. Come in." She held the door

ajar and stepped aside.

Daniel knelt beside the bed, his face lit with joy as he took Mary Anna's hand in his big ones.

"She's so pretty, Daniel. And very strong." Mary Anna pulled the blanket away from the tiny face pressed against her breast. "See."

Daniel did see. "We finally have our daughter. I'm so proud I could pop!" His big fingers brushed the baby's cheek, causing her to turn in confusion to seek another source of nourishment and to howl at the deception.

"She has a big voice for such a little thing," he said, embarrassed at his mistake. They sat quietly for a while just admiring the new baby. The two boys came in to greet their little sister and then were quickly shooed out.

March turned into April, and with it came full spring. Mary Anna felt hale and hearty, and her baby flourished with all the love and attention heaped on her. It was easy to love this child they'd named Elizabeth for Daniel's mother.

She was a true child of the Old Country. A cinnamon sprinkling of freckles powdered her pert nose, and her hair was the deep auburn common to the Irish of Mary Anna's family. From her infancy, she, more than the other children, loved the sound of Daniel's fiddle.

"The melodies of Ireland flow through that child's veins," remarked Daniel as he watched her uncertain baby grin. He drew the bow softly over the strings and delighted anew when she turned her head toward the sound.

The days were almost unbearably sweet for a while, but the talk of secession seeped through the cracks of the logs and under the strong door. It was impossible to ignore. Lincoln was elected. In February Texas had formally seceded from the Union over Sam Houston's strong objections. The time had come to make hard choices.

One evening, Daniel and Caleb sat before the Thornton cabin. Fireflies winked around them, and the soft gurgle of the river added to nature's song.

"What are you going to do now?" Caleb asked. He was sitting in a chair with a rawhide seat, and it squeaked comfortably beneath his weight now and again.

Daniel shook his head. "I honestly don't know. I feel a strong call to help the men with the fighting. Yet I can't stand to leave everything here that we've struggled so hard for."

"With the soldiers gone to fight, there'll soon be no one to help us fight the Comanches." An undercurrent of fear colored Caleb's next words. "You know what can happen if there's no one to defend our women and children."

He and Daniel locked eyes, understanding the consequences of an unchecked Indian raid. Erath County had set up a brigade of men to fill the place of the departed army, but no one knew how effective the group of men would be.

"The South will beat the Union boys pretty quick, if it comes to war," Daniel said confidently. "Question is, where do we stand our ground and what do we defend?"

"I'm planning on staying right here and protecting what I have," Caleb said quietly. "We ain't in it yet. Ain't been no shooting that I know of."

"Then there's no need to make any decisions tonight." Tired, Daniel rose and stretched his long arms. "Got plowing to do tomorrow." He shook hands with Caleb.

"We'll do more talkin' when we know what we're talkin' about."

Daniel nodded in agreement.

Only a few weeks later, Caleb spurred his horse into the yard hurriedly, kicking up puffs of loose dirt.

He accepted Mary Anna's offer to come inside, and she called Daniel in from the fields with the big triangle he'd forged for her. He barely had time to knock the dust off his hat before Caleb spoke.

"It's finally come, Daniel. The South fired on Ft. Sumpter."

"That's means there's war then," he said grimly.

Caleb nodded.

Mary Anna felt sick in the pit of her stomach. "But that doesn't have anything to do with us," she protested.

Both men smiled at her. "We've been trying to decide that for ourselves," Daniel said.

"Waco is getting up an infantry," offered Caleb.

"Kind of in a hurry to get into it, aren't they?" Daniel said. "I think we ought to bide our time and see how the fighting goes."

"But if all of us stay, who will help the South?" argued Caleb. "They'll be needing every man to keep it quick."

"But we can't go traipsing all over the countryside," Daniel argued back. "We could get there after it's over, only to come back here and find we've lost everything we've built." Frustrated, Daniel sipped the coffee Mary Anna had given them.

"Does seem to be an unsolvable problem," Caleb agreed.

"I'm going into town tomorrow and to see what I can find out about the war." Glumly Daniel added, "I'm afraid that either way, we're going to lose a lot."

❧

Daniel said nothing to Mary Anna as they prepared for bed late that night, but she knew he was wrestling with the news. By ignoring it, she had hoped it would go away. After all, the fight was happening far away from them, and Daniel knew how important it was for him to be with his family. She left him to work the issue out in his own mind. Snuggling down in the deep quilts of their bed, she fell asleep praying, *Lord, help Daniel work his way through the problem and give him some peace. Help him to see we need him here. Don't let his love of the South overcome his love for us. Help the South to win their battles without his help. And let it be a brief battle, Lord, for everyone's sake.*

❧

During the next few weeks, Mary Anna heard Daniel say often, "I'm going into town."

"Again? You've just come back." She was cross at his obsession for war news.

"I want to see the _Waco Tribune_. They get their information directly from the eastern newspapers who are there on the scene every day."

At the store he pored over the battered newspaper.

"Hey," said Charlie, "I read where the generals plan their troop movements on what they read in the newspapers. They find out where the enemy is by reading about it!"

"Yeah," added Ted Westmoreland, "Brady and Sullivan and a bunch of other men are taking pictures of the war. They have a big carriage fixed like a darkroom and they're publishing pictures in magazines!"

"I've even heard," Charlie continued, "that some of the people drive out from the towns with picnic baskets to watch from a safe distance. Imagine sitting on the top of a hill eating cold fried chicken and seeing the war taking place below you!"

Daniel relayed all this to Mary Anna. "That's disgusting!" was her only comment.

Still they didn't discuss his leaving.

As the weeks turned into months and almost a year passed, Mary Anna knew time was on her side.

Until one day. She was putting the Dutch oven in the coals to bake their bread when Daniel approached her.

"I'm joining up to fight. I want you to go back to Anderson County. You and the children should be safer there."

Mary Anna looked at him as if the words had absolutely no meaning. "What?" she asked stupidly.

"There's no other way to do it," he said. "I'm joining up. I can't leave my family here at the hands of the Indians."

Anger swept through Mary Anna. "_You_ decided all this without asking me what I thought?" Her voice whispered the words, but they rammed into the walls of the cabin, careening against one another.

He looked at her dumbly, totally taken off guard. He had

been prepared for tears. But not hostility.

"*You* decided what we're going to do!" she repeated.

"Haven't you been thinking about all this?" he asked. "You knew I couldn't let the South fight this thing without helping. Texas has been invaded at Ft. Arbuckle. Colonel Young fought off the Yanks."

"But that's on the Red River," she argued.

He stared into her eyes steadily. "I've got to go, and you know you can't stay here." Softly he added, "I'm afraid the Comanches would get you."

"And you don't think the war will?" she challenged.

"There won't be any more fighting in Texas," he said confidently.

"You don't know that." She turned her back on him, moving to the planked table to clean up her baking mess. Silence was a living thing between them.

Finally Mary Anna spoke. "I don't want to go back. I want to stay here." She looked at him evenly. "And I think you should, too. The South has enough men. It's not our fight. Besides, it'll be over before you can get there."

"What do you mean, it's not our fight?" Now he was angry. It had taken him almost a year to work this thing out, to finally come to the best decision. And his own wife was arguing with him.

"Why? We don't keep any slaves. That should be fought out by the people who do. Our place is here, where we've fought it out with the Indians. Did anyone from the South come to help us?"

"As a matter of fact, they did. Your mother and father being one. And the Wests." He was afraid to move, afraid the logic he had laid down would be ripped apart by her feelings. He had made the choice, and it was the right one. Why was she balking?

Deliberately she turned to face him. "Daniel, I don't want you to go to war. There's enough danger here every day of our lives." She closed her eyes and added, "I know you could be killed any day, but at least I'd know what happened right away. If you go to war, I'll never know what is happening to you. I might never find out why you didn't come home." Tears formed in her eyes. "We promised each other after the trial that we'd never have to be apart again. We promised!"

He crossed the room, taking her in his arms. "I'm not going to get killed in either place," he said against her soft hair. "I have too much to live for. I haven't given you any of those stars I promised yet." He leaned back to look her fully in the face. "This is important to me, Mary Anna. I feel honor bound to fight for a way of life I've always known. The government has no right to tell anyone what they can do on their own land. They need us. They need *me*."

A tiny cold place had begun to form in the corner of Mary Anna's heart. It was next to the one where the death of her children lay. But when she looked into his azure blue eyes glowing with commitment, she felt the will to stand against him slip a little. "But everything is so good here. I don't think I can bear to go off and leave our hard work. . .our little girl out there under the oak tree."

"The baby sleeps in God's arms and our hearts, not in that earth out there," he said gently. "We carry both our lost ones with us wherever we go." He pulled her hard against his broad chest. "And we will build and keep building. We're going to build us an empire. But right now, I must do this. It will weigh heavily on me all my life if I don't." His eyes bore into hers with increasing intensity. "I have to go."

One level of consciousness reached for him, exalted with his honor, and another enlarged the cold spot of dread in her heart. Her mind's eye reached across the days ahead, and all she could see was loneliness and desolation. "I know if I don't give you leave to do this, it will always be between us. I have no right to keep you from doing something that is this important to you. Even the love between us can't protect me from your need for honor."

She heaved a great sigh. "But I don't understand why men must find honor only in war. I would think there would be great honor in building your empire." She looked to see if this made any difference to him. She could see her answer in his handsome face. "When?"

He kissed her with great tenderness. "As soon as we can get packed up. The sooner I go, the sooner I'll be back."

"That's a lie, and you know it. You'll go, but you won't be back soon. War isn't like that. It's long and ugly, and it doesn't always settle the things it's supposed to. I'll pray for you and your safety." She held on to him tightly. "Promise me you'll come back. Even if you're horribly maimed. Come back."

❧

Even the weather seemed to disapprove of what they were doing. It was the end of February, but the day that had begun warm turned hot, the sun glaring at the busy activities below his scorching fingers. The heat made the job of sorting and packing their family belongings harder.

Thunderheads were building up in the west, threatening to put out the sun's heat with a pelting rain guaranteed to drown the snakes out of their holes. Daniel kept a worried eye on the towering clouds that made him work faster. The humidity was building steadily, and his shirt was soaked with perspiration.

Mary Anna looked in consternation at all the goods they had accumulated. Not all of them could go. She was back to taking the necessities of life with her, giving the excess to her friends.

Daniel rode into town the next day to pick up some supplies. He came riding back rapidly and handed her a well-worn letter.

"It's from Father," she read. "They're coming here. He wants Louisa and the rest of the family to live with us while he joins up. According to this letter, they'll be here soon!"

"I should have known. Once a captain, always a captain,"

said Daniel. "That'll work out just fine. You and Louisa can go back and open up a hotel, and we'll ride together to sign up."

Mary Anna bit back the barbed reply on the end of her Irish tongue. Her one consolation was that she wouldn't have to go back alone.

When they revealed their plan to the Wests, Caleb said, "I'm proud you are going, son. I know the South needs men like you. Virginia and I have talked about it, and we both agreed I'm too old to go."

Mary Anna saw the pain in his Southern heart reflected in his eyes, but she also saw the joy in Virginia's eyes at his staying.

"We'll keep an eye on things for you," she said softly. "And the things you've left with me will be waiting for you when you come back."

Mary Anna tried to return the offered smile. She had turned to stone inside.

"Just think," said Virginia, "you're going back to civilization; stores, close neighbors, church. No more Indian raids, and your boys can go to school." In spite of her joy at staying, there was envy at what Mary Anna would have again. "I'm glad Louisa is going with you. It's a long trip."

She put her arms around Mary Anna's stiff body. "The ways of the Lord are mysterious, but He will take care of you now that you know His will."

Mary Anna's voice was low and gruff, "I'm not sure if it's His will or Daniel's will." She sighed tiredly. "I know He will care for us." She gave Virginia a tired smile. "The boys think it's a great adventure. Daniel told Tump he could ride the dun-colored mare."

Tump was close by, and he grinned his toothless six-year-old smile as he fed the mare a handful of soft grass. T.P. was entertaining Elizabeth with a small wooden toy. Everything was the same, and everything was different.

"Virginia, I remember the first time we visited you and Caleb," said Mary Anna.

"I do, too. That was such a happy day for me." She gave her friend a loving smile. "You've given me a lot of happy days."

"It's not going to be the same without you." Something suspiciously like tears were forming in Mary Anna's eyes. "What will I do without you?"

"Oh, I 'spect you'll find a lot of friends in town."

"It'll be so strange living in a town. Sometimes I think of all the good things you mentioned. But I have the strangest feeling of being crowded, living so close to everyone. Odd, isn't it?"

Virginia nodded in agreement. "You going to be all right for money?"

"Daniel said he'd send me his army pay. It's thirteen dollars a month. I'll get a job until Father can get his own hotel. We'll be fine. I'll have my garden, and Louisa is planning to raise a whole flock of chickens."

"It sounds like y'all have thought of everything."

They both knew they were running out of small talk, and they couldn't bear to say the things they wanted to say to each other.

"It's best we go so you can get on with your packin'."

"I'll write," Mary Anna promised.

Virginia laughed. "I'll watch for that letter. It'll be almost as good as a visit."

"Virginia, stay safe." Mary Anna's brow puckered with concern. "If things get too bad out here, come to Tennessee Colony. You'll always have a place to stay. The future is so muddled right now with the war and all. If you need help, come to me."

Virginia couldn't get her voice past the hard knot of sadness locked in her throat. She hugged Mary Anna, blew a kiss to the children, and climbed up beside Caleb in the wagon. "God bless," she whispered as they headed the horses back to their cabin.

Most of the packing was done by the time they turned in for the night. They had a cold supper, and the only conversation came from the children. Neither Daniel nor Mary Anna could find anything to say.

Mary Anna ached to tell Daniel not to go.

Daniel ached to remind Mary Anna of why he had to.

When they climbed into their bed, Daniel finally said, "Your folks should be here tomorrow. If they're not, we'll leave them a note and go on. The weather is very changeable right now, and I don't want to leave in a rain storm."

Mary Anna prayed for a rain storm to end all rain storms, but when she climbed wearily out of her side of the bed, the new day was clear and bright.

She couldn't afford to waste this day. She would squeeze every piece of time like a miser giving out coins. This would be her last day with Daniel. She looked back at their bed. Daniel appeared to be sleeping. On silent feet, she went back and slid under the covers with him.

"I'm glad you came back," he whispered as he gathered her up in his arms.

"It's still cold out there," she whispered as she snuggled closer to his body.

"I'm going to miss you more than I can say, my love."

"And I, you," she breathed.

He stroked her hair with a practiced hand and ran his fingers across her mouth in the way that made her tingle with delight.

Mary Anna knew that if she took advantage of his desire to make love to her, she might have a chance to talk him out of going. He was vulnerable. She could beg him not to break the bonds of love that held them together. Remind him that there was no way to know when they could be together again like this. She could use his desire to make him stay. But she chose to make it the most memorable time of their lives, a celebration of their love that would endure even a wartime separation.

And when they lay in each other's arms spent, she stroked his face with her fingertips to memorize every line. She kissed his mouth a hundred times to make her lips remember his. She molded herself to his body in an effort to be able to recall its feel in the lonely times to come.

All day she watched him with covert eyes, saving every scrap of his voice, his walk, his face, and his hands. She watched him all during the favorite breakfast she prepared for him. She watched while he played with the boys and little Betty.

Daniel felt Mary Anna's eyes on his every move. He was watching her in the same way. He was a man tied on two horses going in opposite directions. Duty called him. His love for Mary Anna and the children ripped at his heart.

He had thought one or the other would finally win out and he would be at peace with his decision, but the war inside him raged as hard as the one to which he was going.

Why did he have this compelling need to help the South? He hated himself for it. But it wouldn't go away. The South had sent out a call for help, and he couldn't ignore it. The shining honor he called his manhood was being challenged. Not to go would dishonor himself and his family. But when he looked at Mary Anna, he felt his will begin to slip. It would be so much easier and happier to stay with her.

With great deliberation he prepared himself to leave. As he was tying on his saddle bags and bedroll, he saw the cloud of dust coming from the distance. "I think your folks are here, Mary Anna," he called to the cabin.

She came outside with a slow step to watch the dust get closer.

There were no excited exchanges of greetings. Louisa was cold and withdrawn. Mary Anna was numb. Only the boys were excited to see their grandparents again.

Daniel took Mary Anna in his arms one last time. She tried desperately not to cry. She summoned strength from deep within to meet the sweet passion of his lips on hers for the last time.

And then he was astride his tall horse.

A strange swelling of pride that she was able to send her man into battle with clear, bright eyes filled Mary Anna's soul. She stood as tall as she could and waved him out of sight, wearing her frontier eyes until she was sure Daniel could no longer see her. Then she cried quietly to herself, fearing the tears would upset the children who had so proudly sent their father and grandfather off to fight the war to save the South.

Lord, keep both of them safe and bring them home soon. Give us all the courage to face this terrible time of testing. I don't know who is right, the Union or the South, but let it end quickly. Spare our men, please, Lord. Daniel belongs to You now. Bring him back home so he can live out the kind of life You'd be proud of. You can use him to build more of Your kingdom. Lord God of all creation, I beg You to bring back my love to me.

And she poured out her tears as sacrifices to God for Daniel's safe return.

A Letter To Our Readers

Dear Reader:

In order that we might better contribute to your reading enjoyment, we would appreciate your taking a few minutes to respond to the following questions. When completed, please return to the following:

Rebecca Germany, Editor
Heartsong Presents
P.O. Box 719
Uhrichsville, Ohio 44683

1. Did you enjoy reading *Dreams of the Pioneers*?
   - ❑ Very much. I would like to see more books
     by this author!
   - ❑ Moderately
     I would have enjoyed it more if _____
     _____

2. Are you a member of **Heartsong Presents**? ❑Yes ❑No
   If no, where did you purchase this book? _____
   _____

3. What influenced your decision to purchase this
   book? (Check those that apply.)

❑ Cover	❑ Back cover copy
❑ Title	❑ Friends
❑ Publicity	❑ Other_____

4. How would you rate, on a scale from 1 (poor) to 5
   (superior), **Heartsong Presents'** new cover design?_____

5. On a scale from 1 (poor) to 10 (superior), please rate the following elements.

      ___Heroine   ___Plot

      ___Hero   ___Inspirational theme

      ___Setting   ___Secondary characters

6. What settings would you like to see covered in **Heartsong Presents** books?_____

_____

_____

7. What are some inspirational themes you would like to see treated in future books?_____

_____

_____

8. Would you be interested in reading other **Heartsong Presents** titles?   ❏ Yes   ❏ No

9. Please check your age range:
    ❏ Under 18   ❏ 18-24   ❏ 25-34
    ❏ 35-45   ❏ 46-55   ❏ Over 55

10. How many hours per week do you read? _____

Name _____

Occupation _____

Address _____

City_____ State_____ Zip _____

VeraLee Wiggins

THE FORERUNNERS

_*Heartbreak Trail*—While Rachel Butler gains in strength physically traversing the legendary Oregon Trail, her heart struggles to keep pace. Reverend James Richards is the handsomest man on the wagon train, but the young physician, Tom Dorland, has a quiet appeal Rachel can't deny. HP76 $2.95

_ *Martha My Own*—Martha's journey on the Oregon Trail ends in the Washington Territory where hard times continue to plague her. Rescued more than once by the heroic and faithful Abram Noble, she and Abram resort to a marriage in name only so she can survive. HP83 $2.95

_*Abram My Love*—Abe Noble's love for Martha Lawford knows no bounds. Yet their tacit agreement—a marriage of convenience, one in name only—denies such feelings. Together as they battle the forces of nature in the early years of Washington State, will Abram and Martha realize the forces of love? HP92 $2.95

_*Misplaced Angel*—Rachel Dorland lives by this Scripture: In as much as ye have done it unto one of the least of these my brethren, ye have done it unto me. Soon Rachel finds herself caring for seven children, plus her own. Rachel is so tired she can barely think, but how can this misplaced angel turn away her Lord? HP128 $2.95

Presents

Heart♥ng Presents
Love Stories Are Rated G!

That's for godly, gratifying, and of course, great! If you love a thrilling love story, but don't appreciate the sordidness of some popular paperback romances, **Heartsong Presents** is for you. In fact, **Heartsong Presents** is the *only inspirational romance book club*, the only one featuring love stories where Christian faith is the primary ingredient in a marriage relationship.

Sign up today to receive your first set of four, never before published Christian romances. Send no money now; you will receive a bill with the first shipment. You may cancel at any time without obligation, and if you aren't completely satisfied with any selection, you may return the books for an immediate refund!

Imagine. . .four new romances every four weeks—two historical, two contemporary—with men and women like you who long to meet the one God has chosen as the love of their lives. . .all for the low price of $9.97 postpaid.

To join, simply complete the coupon below and mail to the address provided. **Heartsong Presents** romances are rated G for another reason: They'll arrive *Godspeed!*
